KW-483-182

REVENGE!

REVENGE!

The third adventure in the O'Sullivans of the S.A.S. series

by

Leo Kessler

writing as

John Kerrigan

This first world edition published in Great Britain by
SEVERN HOUSE PUBLISHERS LTD of
9–15 High Street, Sutton, Surrey SM1 1DF.
First published in the USA 1996 by
SEVERN HOUSE PUBLISHERS INC of
595 Madison Avenue, New York, NY 10022.

Copyright © 1996 by John Kerrigan.
All rights reserevd.
The moral right of the author has been asserted.

British Library Cataloguing in Publication Data
Kerrigan, John
    Revenge! (O'Sullivans of the SAS : bk. 3)
    1.English fiction – 20th century
    I. Title II. Kessler, Leo, 1926–
    823.9′14[F]

    ISBN 0-7278-4928-X

All situations in this publication are fictitious and
any resemblance to living persons is purely coincidental.

Typeset by Hewer Text Composition Services, Edinburgh.
Printed and bound in Great Britain by
Creative Print and Design Ltd, Ebbw Vale, Wales.

LONDON BOROUGH
OF SUTTON
PUBLIC LIBRARIES

018124067
FEB 1997
F

'An eye for an eye . . . a tooth for a tooth.'
The Bible

CONGRESSIONAL RECORD – SENATE
April 26, 1996

ALLEGED SWISS COLLABORATION WITH THE NAZIS AND THE SMUGGLING OF GERMAN-LOOTED PROPERTY TO ARGENTINA.

MR D'AMATO:'Mr President, I rise today to discuss an issue that continues to trouble me, namely that of the role played by the Swiss banks and their continued retention of assets belonging to European Jews and others before and during World War Two.

'A document from the State Department entitled *Nazi and Fascist capital in Latin America*, dated March 28, 1945, found at the National Archives, details Nazi capital infiltration of Latin and South America. Yet within the report there are sections which explain the role of the Swiss bankers in helping to secret Nazi assets out of Europe. At this time, Mr President, I ask unanimous consent that this report be printed in the RECORD.'

The relevant part of the report states:

1

'Accusations have also been voiced that Nazi German capital is escaping in Swiss diplomatic pouches, probably without the knowledge of the Swiss Federal Government because of the Federal Government's practice of entrusting diplomatic missions to bankers and businessmen travelling to the Western Hemisphere.

'If this is true it suggests that Swiss bankers might have directly to get Nazi assets out of Europe into Latin and South America. This relevation could lead to serious questions about the sincerity of Swiss bankers with regard to Jewish assets in their possession as well as those of the Nazis. Where did all of the money go? That is what the Banking Committee will try to find out.'

Senator D'Amato need to have no fears on that score. Admittedly some smaller sums of Nazi gold did get through to Switzerland in the last year of the war. But when in the autumn of 1945 a determined attempt was made by a strange collection of Nazis, black American soldiers, a white traitor, and what was left of the German underground organisation, the Werewolves, to get the vast bulk of the German State Bank's bullion out of Occupied Germany into Switzerland, they had not reckoned with the O'Sullivans of the Special Air Service. Just two of them, plus six other brave troopers of the SAS, stopped that shipment of Nazi gold which would have been used to create a Fourth Reich. More, they paid back a debt of blood. That is what this story is about – *THE REVENGE!*

John Kerrigan, Colmar, Alsace, 1996

2

PART ONE

The End Of The SAS

Chapter One

Over in the port of Bremen, the heavy guns crashed. Huge pillars of black smoke rose to the flat April sky. The high, hysterical bursts of Spandau fire were followed by the more sedate spurts of Bren light-machine-guns as the soldiers of the British Thirty Corps pushed ever closer to the centre of the ruined German city. Now and again in the artillery pauses the waiting SAS troopers could hear angry shouts and the hoarse commands of NCOs and officers urging the infantry to press home their attack.

But the ambushers had little time for the attacking infantry. They concentrated on the slow-flowing river which led out of Bremen to the sea. Intelligence had warned them what to expect when the German Naval High Command realised the city was going to fall to the British. That would happen this very day, Thirty Corps HQ had confirmed that. The victims should be making their appearance soon.

Second Lieutenant Miles O'Sullivan, commanding the anti-tank troop, 18 years old and six months out of Eton, but already holder of the Military Cross, scanned the smoke-shrouded river with his glasses. On the other side a crane had suffered a direct hit and lay crumpled in a mess of grotesquely twisted steel on the quayside. Next to it a dead German sniper lay sprawled in a star of his own blood. Passing the dead body there was an old woman, tugging a cart laden high with her pathetic bits and pieces and trying to flee the dying city before the end came. One of the younger troopers raised his rifle eagerly, but Sergeant Smith, the veteran, swiftly knocked down the muzzle growling, "Take it easy, sonny. Leave the poor old biddy alone. She's got problems enough as it is, poor old cow!"

"Yes Sarge," the young trooper said a little crestfallen. "I wasn't thinking."

"Ner, yer weren't," Smith 175, as he had been known ever since he had first joined the SAS back in the desert to differentiate him from all the other Smiths in the elite regiment, said. "That's why—"

"Knock it off," Miles O'Sullivan cut in urgently. "I think I can hear something, Smithie."

All eyes turned to stare up the smoke-shrouded River Weser. The gunners tensed behind the shields of their 6-pounder anti-tank guns. They had never had an opportunity like this before and probably never would have again. If it worked, it was going to be something that they could tell their grandkids about – if they lived that long.

Miles, his boyish face strained and set, could definitely make out a throbbing noise coming down from the direction of the city. He had never heard a submarine's diesels before, but he guessed they would sound like that. "Lads," he said, whispering for some reason or all other, "I think it's them. They're doing a bunk, as Intelligence said they would."

Hastily the loaders rammed home the armour-piercing shells and tapped the gun layers on the shoulder to indicate that the weapon loaded. The gun

6

layers squatted on the gun-trail and peered through their little telescopic sights in anticipation. It wouldn't be long now and suddenly all was tense anticipation and controlled excitement.

Again Miles O'Sullivan swept the river's surface with his glasses. For a moment or two the steady throbbing noise of engines was drowned by the crash and thick crump of a salvo of heavy shells landing in the ruined city. Then there was the sound again – and how it was coming ever closer. Hastily, excitedly, the young SAS officer adjusted the focus of his binoculars.

Suddenly there it was! A lean grey shape sliding into the bright calibrated circles of glass. "It's them, lads," Miles O'Sullivan shouted. "Stand by to open fire when I give the word!" He peered through the glasses again. There was another of those lean grey shapes which had been the scourge of the British Merchant Navy during the middle years of the war, when the U-boat packs had forced Britain almost to her knees. Now that the war in Europe was nearly over, Miles knew he should feel some compassion for these German sailors trying to escape from the inevitable, but he could not. He remembered the months in 1941 and 1942 when he and the rest of his fellow pupils at Eton lived off near-starvation rations.

Behind them there was a sudden roar. A goggled dispatch rider in his ankle-length coat skidded to a halt. He brushed the dust from his face and hurried to where the officer crouched, already feeling into the leather pouch slung across his stomach. He saluted and snapped above the angry crack and bang of small-arms fire in the dying city: "Message for you, sir. Urgent." He handed Miles the folded buff form and waited, wondering why these tough-looking troopers, with the winged dagger badge of the SAS on their maroon berets, were crouched so tensely behind the three 6-pounder anti-tank guns. There were no Jerry tanks on the other side of the river as far as he could see. In fact, Old Jerry was about finished, everybody knew that.

Hastily, knowing that the U-boats were slowly getting within range, Miles O'Sullivan scanned the official signal, marked 'Most Immediate'. He read *'Secret, all offensive ops will cease from receipt of this signal. Orders will be given to cease fire 0800 hrs tomorrow, Saturday 28 April. Full terms of local German surrender arranged today at 21 Army Grp front. Emphasise these provision apply solely 21 Army Grp. ACK, DOP. Emergency. R. M. Belchem.'*

Miles flushed angrily. He stuffed the message roughly into the pocket of his battledress.

The DR looked at him curiously. "Any answer, sir?" he enquired.

"No!" Miles snapped. "Because you haven't delivered that signal *yet!*"

Puzzled, the man looked at him. "What, sir?" he asked.

"You heard! You'll deliver the signal in about 15 minutes time."

"But I've already delivered it, sir," the DR stuttered.

Miles O'Sullivan knew he had no more time for further discussion. He pointed to a wrecked shed to the rear of the anti-tank guns. "Go in that shed, Corporal, and you'll find it packed high with Bremen's best beer – Haemlingen's Beck. Help yourself to as much as you can drink and then come back here. I'll acknowledge receipt of the signal then."

The DR walked away slowly, attracted by the

8

prospect of good German beer, but muttering to himself that all "yon SAS blokes were as nutty as bleeding fruit cakes."

The waiting SAS men ignored the mutterings of the puzzled dispatch rider. They concentrated on their targets: three U-boats now gliding through the fog of war like silent grey ghosts, the throb of their engines barely audible.

Mike O'Sullivan allowed himself a careful grin. "Smithie," he said to the giant ex-Guardsman, "we've got them by the short and curlies. This'll be a first for the SAS – shooting up some Nazi subs. Old Paddy," he referred to the CO of the 1st SAS Regiment, "will be green with envy when he hears!"

Smith 175 shared his grin. "That he will, Boss. We've shot up planes by the score, even a couple of goods trains in Eyetie land, but never a sub. *Here they come!*" his words ended on a hectic note. The submarines were now definitely within range, every detail of their superstructure clearly visible and they were all still flying that hated crooked cross of the Third Reich. They were coming out not to surrender but to fight and Miles O'Sullivan, the third man of his family to serve in the SAS*, was prepared to give them that fight, and more.

"All right, lads," he called above the roar of heavy guns in Bremen, "Range 200 yards. Fire at will! *FIRE!*"

The gleeful SAS gunners needed no urging. They spun their little anti-tank cannons round. The long, slim barrels targetted the unsuspecting Germans. The

---

* See John Kerrigan: *Kill Rommel* and *Surprise Attack* for further details.

9

first gun layer ripped back his firing rod. The 6-pounder bucked and angry cherry-red flame erupted from its muzzle. For one brief instant Miles caught a glimpse of the white blur which was an armour-piercing tracer shell and then it was gone, speeding flatly across the surface of the river towards the leading U-boat.

There was the hollow boom of steel striking steel. The U-boat reeled. For a moment its radio mast seemed to touch the water. Suddenly, startlingly, a great gleaming silver star appeared on the side of the conning-tower as the periscope came tumbling down in a mess of wrecked metal.

The second gun thundered into life. In the same instant that the U-boat's gun crew raced out of the battered conning-tower for the deck gun, it disappeared in a burst of scarlet flame and molten metal. The gun crew were ripped from the deck like flies being swatted by a giant hand. The U-boat came to a sudden stop, listing badly to port.

Hastily the SAS gunners reloaded and turned their attention to the next U-boat as the Bren-gunners started to spray the deck of the crippled U-boat with tracer, keeping the crew cowering behind the shelter of the badly damaged conning tower.

The rounds from the three anti-tank guns slapped into the next boat at close range. This U-boat rocked and trembled like a live thing. Blue sparks crackled along the deck as its wireless mast came tumbling down. In the conning tower, the white-capped skipper clapped his hand to his face and reeled back, the flesh of his face slipping down to his chin like molten red sealing wax.

Still the SAS gunners showed no mercy. It had been a tough war for them. All of them knew, even the youngest recruit, that should they fall into German hands they would be executed on the spot. Hitler had ordered that personally and in the past year there had been too many of the 1st SAS Brigade shot out of hand by the Germans without trial or mercy. Now they took their revenge, feeling no remorse for the young German sailors being slaughtered so cruelly.

But an end to the killing was coming. On the deck of the third U-boat emerging from the smoke wafting across the River Weser, the black and white banner of the German *Kriegsmarine* was being hauled down hurriedly by a panic-stricken group of young German submariners. In its place a white flag, which seemed to consist of a pair of men's drawers, was being hoisted on the flag-pole.

"Christ all-bleeding mighty!" Smith 175 gasped. "They're running up fanny's drawers . . . They're surrendering, Boss!"

The Germans were indeed.

Five minutes later the two damaged submarines and the undamaged U-boat were drawing up at the quayside, their young crews sullen and truculent as the SAS ambush team trained their Bren guns on them warily, wearing big, happy grins on their faces as they thought of the looting to come. The Yanks, who would soon take over Bremen, would pay a fortune for the Lugers and the like that the German U-boat officers had at their waists.

Miles O'Sullivan nodded to Smith 175 and snapped, "All right, Smithie. Start disarming the buggers, but you see that big Jerry naval flag?"

"Sir?"

"I want it. It's going to be my personal souvenir of the war in Europe before they send us to the Far

11

East to have our head blown off by the slant-eyed devils."

"Yessir!"

Five minutes later it was all over. The crews of the three U-boats, sullen and resentful, were lined up along the quayside, hands on their heads, while a triumphant Miles O'Sullivan looked happily at the newly captured flag.

It was just then that the DR came staggering out of the warehouse, carrying a half-empty bottle of Beck's beer, swaying badly as he did so. The SAS men roared with laughter at the sight and Smith 175 suggested with mock earnestness, "I think you'd better walk home, sonny."

The DR made an obscene gesture with his free hand. "Don't you ferking SAS men know that the ferking war in Europe is over? Why go and get yesens frigging killed now?"

But for the survivors of the 1st SAS Regiment the war, now a war in the shadows, was just about to begin . . .

Chapter Two

Things were moving at the headquarters of the 1st SAS, a school-house on the outskirts of Bremen. It was clear that the drunken dispatch rider was right – the war in Europe was about over. Jeeps filled with grinning SAS troopers were leading in long columns of dejected and dirty German infantry, down the roads leading to the HQ. Someone was moaning plaintively, "But what am I gonna do with the sods? There's only four of us, sir, and I've got a thousand of the sods wanting to surrender! What am I gonna do?"

An excited Miles pushed his way through the Germans, still carrying his captured flag, full of the news he wanted to spring on his uncle, Rory O'Sullivan, the regimental adjutant, that they had just taken three German U-boats. He thrust himself into the corridor, still adorned with childish scrawls and pictures bearing legends in German script that, '*Pas ist mein Haus . . . Hier wohne ich*' and so on, which seemed out of place in this community of hard-bitten men with their tough, weather-beaten faces under their maroon berets, who hurried back and forth carrying out their military duties.

Hurriedly, Miles knocked on the door of the classroom bearing the legend 'Regimental Orderly Room.'

13

The familiar voice of his Uncle Rory barked, "Come!"

Miles went in, clicked to attention and saluted his uncle, noting as he did so that Rory was obviously in pain again, where his foot had been blown away six months before in Strasbourg. His face was pale and there was a set, tight look about his mouth as if he were trying hard not to groan aloud with the pain. "Hello Miles! Where's the fire?" Rory asked.

Despite the look on his uncle's face, Miles O'Sullivan couldn't contain himself. "I've just captured three German subs in the Weser. I think that's a first for the SAS, sir, don't you? I mean we're not naval types . . ."

He didn't finish the sentence, for he could see that his uncle wasn't particularly interested. "Is there anything wrong, sir?" he said after a few moments.

Rory O'Sullivan did not reply for what seemed a long time. It was as if he were preoccupied. Outside, someone was yelling, "*Los*, you German bastards, *mak schnell!*" while a cook, busy peeling a dixie of potatoes, was happily singing, "*There was ham, ham, mixed up with the jam in the quartermaster's stores . . . I cannot see . . . I' didn't bring me specs with me . . .*"

Finally Rory broke his heavy, brooding silence: "The Brig" – he meant the commander of the 1st SAS Brigade, Brigadier Mike Calvert – "is coming from Oldenburg. He's just telephoned Paddy Mayne to announce himself." He paused and bit his bottom lip with a worried look on his drawn face. "I think he's the bearer of bad tidings, now that the war in Europe is about over bar the shouting."

Miles dropped the formal 'sir'. Instead, he asked, "What kind of bad tidings, Rory?"

"For the regiment."

14

The young officer looked puzzled. "How do you mean? There's still the war in the Far East. No doubt they'll be sending us there in due course. You know what the troopers say – "BLA* stands for 'Burma Looms Ahead'."

BRITISH ARMY OF THE RHINE

His uncle was unconvinced. "You know, Miles, a lot of people in high office, including the War House, don't like the SAS. They say Monty himself is against formations like ours. Private armies they call us and the commandos. They're only too eager to get rid of us, have us assimilated back into regular infantry regiments."

Miles O'Sullivan looked at his uncle aghast. "You can't mean that, Rory, can you? Honestly!"

"I can," his uncle replied solemnly. "I mean we are the newest regiment in the British Army, our founder David Stirling is still in a Jerry POW camp and we've got no powerful regimental colonels with influence at court backing us. No, they'll give us the chop if they can get away with it." He shook his head a little wearily.

Outside, the singing trooper suddenly stopped in the middle of his monotonous dirge and slammed to attention. "Morning, sir! Good to see you, sir."

Rory reached for his cane and his beret. "That'll be the Brig. Come on, let's get outside to welcome him. Mad Mike's a stickler for discipline."

Hurriedly he went out, tugging on his beret, his 'wooden foot' as he called it, creaking audibly as he did so, followed by his nephew.

Brigadier Mike Calvert was standing on the running board of his looted German Army Mercedes, watched

---

* The official name of the British Army fighting in Germany: 'British Liberation Army'.

cagily by his bodyguard, armed with a tommy-gun. He was talking earnestly to Colonel Paddy Mayne, commanding officer of the 1st SAS. He was dwarfed by the giant Irishman, but the Brigadier didn't look intimidated by the tough Irishman who had joined the SAS back in the desert in order not to be court-martialled for having chased his superior officer out of the mess with a naked bayonet.

Calvert, Miles told himself, was a very tough man himself with that powerful simian look of his and arms that seemed to reach to the ground. He had fought the Japs in Malaya, killing several with his bare hands, when Miles had still been at prep school. He had dropped behind enemy lines with Wingate's Chindits and had made an epic 1,000-mile march back to India with what was left of his men. No, he concluded, not even Paddy Mayne could intimidate the Brig.

Rory O'Sullivan snapped to attention and saluted. "Good-morning, sir! Hope all is well."

Calvert gave them that deceptive soft smile of his and said, "Ah, the O'Sullivans! The whole regiment seems to be made up of O'Sullivans, they pop up all over the place." He nodded at the new ribbon of the Military Cross on Miles' tunic and commented, "Well earned gong there, young Miles. Good show!"

"Thank you, sir." Miles felt himself going red with embarrassment.

"All right, gentlemen," Calvert said, "let's go inside. I've got some news for you."

Rory O'Sullivan flashed his nephew a significant look. The boy shrugged, wondering if his uncle had been right after all.

They pushed their way through the captured Germans, who were being prodded by the tough SAS troopers to get out of the way, with "Move yer arses, you Jerries! You Herringfolk" – the troopers meant the *Herrenvolk* – "have had yer day now."

"True, very true," Calvert commented, as if he might be well speaking to himself. "At times I thought we'd never beat the devils. Now we've done it – and there, gentlemen, is where the rub starts, as Shakespeare once said."

Minutes later they were seated in what had once been the headmaster's office with a photograph of Hitler still hanging on the wall, though the glass had been smashed and someone had scrawled a rude comment about Hitler's parents on the wall beneath it.

Although it was only ten in the morning, all of them were drinking whisky. It had been a long and tough six weeks since they had crossed the Rhine at the end of March 1945 and they felt they needed a drink whatever the time.

"Well, gentlemen," Calvert announced, "Monty's currently negotiating the surrender of all German troops in Northern Germany, Denmark and Norway, plus Holland. In fact I think he'll do the Yanks one in the eye and get the whole bang-shoot to surrender to the British Army."

He lifted his glass and Paddy did the same, saying, "I'll drink to that, Brig."

Obediently they all drained their glasses and, being the youngest there, Miles reached for the Scotch and refilled them. Again they sipped their drinks and waited for Calvert to tell them the reason for his visit to the 1st SAS Regiment. Outside in the direction of Bremen the roar of the guns was beginning to diminish as if to

17

signify that the war in Europe was really coming to an end. Finally Calvert cleared his throat and said, "Let me give you the bad news first. I'm being returned to my regiment and after we've collared the Germans still up in Norway, all three regiments are to be sent to the UK."

"Burma?" Paddy Mayne asked eagerly.

Calvert shook his head. "'Fraid not, Paddy. No, we're going to be stood down. That's what the powers-that-be want. It's the end of the SAS, well for most of it anyway."

Miles caught that qualification. The others didn't. Paddy slammed his huge fist like a small steam shovel against the side of the German headmaster's desk and snarled, "The buggers! They got us in the end!"

Calvert, who was a regular soldier while all the rest were 'Hostilities Only' men, nodded sympathetically. "Yes, they did. You can't fight the War House, you know. They've been doing this sort of thing for 300-odd years. You can't imagine the power that some of those brasshats have." He shrugged those apelike shoulders of his. "No matter. However, there is one slight ray of hope for some of you. I have been asked to select a few key officers and men to be sent back to London to be briefed for a special mission."

"What kind of mission, sir?" Rory asked eagerly, while Paddy Mayne sat there, slumped in gloom.

"'Fraid I can't clue you in at this stage. It's a sort of needs-to-know kind of thing. Old Churchill's behind it, apparently."

"*Mr Churchill?*" they exclaimed as one.

Calvert nodded. "Yes, he's got a soft spot for the SAS, you know, even though we kicked his son Randolph out of the Regiment. Besides there are several scores to be

18

paid off after what the Jerries have been doing to our chaps they captured ever since that secret commando order that Hitler issued back in 1943."

Mayne nodded grimly. "Yes, you're right there, Brig. I didn't believe the Huns would do that sort of thing, especially when our chaps they captured were wearing uniform. After all, they weren't spies. But they did. They shot them—"

"And worse," Rory O'Sullivan added grimly. "Remember last year? Those poor chaps we found in Alsace. The things they did to those fellows don't bear thinking about."

Mayne slammed his big fist against the desk once more. "If I could get my paws on that damned Dr Barsch or whatever the name of the chief torturer was he wouldn't be in the land of the living for very long, I can assure you of of that."

Miles looked at the veterans' faces. Big tough men, their features were a mixture of anger, sadness and frustration and he told himself that he had had a good war in comparison with theirs. They had seen defeat – and worse.

Brigadier Calvert drained his whisky and immediately Miles reached out for the bottle and refilled their glasses. "So, Paddy," Calvert said carefully, as if he knew all about Mayne's explosive temper and didn't want to upset him, "I know you've done your bit and are due for demob." He pointed his glass at Paddy's beribboned chest. "Four military crosses in four years is not bad going even for the SAS. What do you say? Do you want to take charge of the party that's staying on?"

Paddy Mayne frowned. After a moment he said, "No, Brig. I don't think I do. I can't stand seeing the

Regiment being broken up like this. I think I'll take my bowler and brolly and go back to soliciting."

Calvert smiled carefully. For the life of him, he told himself, he couldn't imagine the Irish giant, who had boxed and played rugby for Ireland, ever again taking up his pre-war profession as a provincial solicitor. "All right, Paddy, I can understand. Going back to my old regiment the Royal Engineers is going to be very tame too after the SAS. But I'm a regular. I've got to consider my career."

"Sir." It was Rory O'Sullivan.

"Yes, Rory?"

"Well, sir, if you're prepared to take on somebody with a wooden foot and let him pick his own team, I'm your man. There's a certain Dr Barsch I'd like to meet up with in the very near future." Rory's normally good-humoured face was set and hard, the blue eyes suddenly angry. "The 1st SAS Regiment has a score to pay off in that quarter . . .!"

Chapter Three

They had spotted him immediately, as the French Sherman tanks opened up with their 75mm cannons trying to stop the Germans fleeing across the Rhine bridge back to Germany. All had been chaos and confusion. Panick-stricken German civilians, soldiers throwing away their weapons in their haste to escape. French snipers leaning out of the upper floors of the half-timbered waterfront houses and shooting their long-time occupiers with cold-blooded precision, speeding them on their way from Strasbourg back to the Reich at last.

Rory O'Sullivan had stood up in the front of the jeep as Smith 175 twisted and turned madly to get through the frantic mob heading for the bridge. On the other side they could already see the German engineers running back and forth carrying crates of high explosive, while an officer with a little trumpet and flag stood by, anxiously waiting for the signal which would indicate that an explosion was about to take place.*

"They're gonna blow the sod, sir!" Smith 175 yelled wildly.

"Keep going, Smithie!" Rory yelled back. They had

* See John Kerrigan: *Surprise Attack* for further details.

21

come all this way to Strasbourg, battling their way through the snow-bounded mountains, to get that swine Barsch. He wasn't going to be cheated of his prey at this late stage.

Their tyres pulped the pickled arms and legs which Barsch had provided for the crazy professor of the University of Strasbourg from the local concentration camp at Natzweiler. Instinctively Rory O'Sullivan knew that the men driving the truck from which these gory, hideous 'specimens' were dropping were the ones he sought. Now he prepared for that one last action which would bring the 1st SAS's long quest to an end.

They slammed into one of the Gestapo men, who had been reaching for his Schmeisser in one last desperate attempt to stop them. He yelled with pain, dropping to one knee, blood jetting in a bright red arc from his shattered leg.

Rory's pistol flashed into his hand. He curled his finger menacingly round the trigger. The man looked up at him, his fat, ugly face filled with despair, fear in his eyes. How many times had he been in the same position as the Englishman was now. *He* had never shown any mercy on his victims as they had pleaded with him. Now it was his turn. He twisted and wrung his hands in the classic pose of supplication, tears of pain and self-pity streaming down his cheeks.

"*Nicht schiessen, Kamerad!*" he whined, the tears running down his cheeks like opaque pearls. "Don't shoot . . . *bitte!*"

"I'm not your damned *Kamerad,*" Rory had snapped angrily and without pity. He cocked the hammer of his pistol. "*Wo . . . Dokter Barsch . . . schnell?* Or you're

22

a frigging dead man." His knuckles whitened as he applied the pressure on his trigger.

Desperately the Gestapo man pointed to the barricade which the German military police had thrown across the bridge so that deserters wouldn't be able to flee to the safety of the Reich. "*Der . . . der mit der Brille*," he gasped, relief in his ashen face for he knew he had been saved for a little while. "*Da.*"

"The one with the glasses," Roy snapped at Smith 175, "that's the murdering shit, Smithie . . . Come on, step on it!"

"But they're gonna blow the bridge, Boss," Smith protested again, desperately. "It's ruddy dangerous."

Rory O'Sullivan ignored the urgent warning. He remembered the two mutilated bodies of the young SAS troopers they had found a month earlier, one with his penis sliced off and thrust into his gaping dead mouth. That had been the work of Dr Barsch and his thugs. He had to be punished for that abomination. "Keep it going, dammit it!" he snarled harshly. "He's not going to get away!"

Smith frowned, but threw the jeep into gear once more. They rolled forward, fighting their way through the panic-stricken mob of fleeing German civilians and soldiers.

On the other side of the Rhine, the engineer officer blew his little trumpet and yelled, "Prepared to blow!" Most of the first bunch of refugees had cleared the bridge, the rest would have to be sacrificed. A fat bespectacled officer, running all out, chubby arms working like pistons, was also half-way across. He'd make it as well, the engineer officer thought as he raised his flag.

To the engineer officer's right, the sergeant spat on

his horny palms and took hold of the wooden plunger of the detonator box. Next to him the others turned their keys which armed the boxes and did the same. The engineer raised his hand and began counting off the seconds. "*One* . . ."

Desperately, Rory sprang from the jeep, which was unable to proceed any farther. He vaulted over the barricade. A military policeman tried to stop him but Rory kicked him in the crotch. He reeled back gagging and holding his testicles, his false teeth bulging absurdly from his gaping mouth.

"*Boss* . . . *sir!*" Smith 175 yelled after him as on the other side of the great border river, the engineer officer snapped, "*Three!*" The big Sergeant let the words die on his lips. It was already too late.

The men at the detonators plunged home the wooden handles. Almost instantly angry little blue and red sparks started to erupt beneath the Kehl Bridge. Little puffs of white smoke burst through the cracks in the stone work. Now, with ever increasing violence, the bridge started to sway and tremble. There was a deep, ominous throaty rumbling, then a sinister crackling sound ran the length of the bridge.

With the last of his strength, his heart seemingly threatening to burst out of his rib cage, the fat German, with the pince-nez like those of his evil master, *Reichsführer SS* Himmler, threw himself forward. He dived for the safety of the opposite bank, sprawling out in the mud and reeds like a high diver who had missed the water.

Behind him Rory O'Sullivan felt the bridge giving beneath his running feet. Now he was pelting along like a drunken man, trying desperately to keep his balance as the tarmac cracked and swayed great gaps

24

appearing in its surface. For a while he seemed to be running uphill. Then in a change of direction the swaying bridge dipped and he was trying to keep himself from falling downwards.

Suddenly the inevitable happened.

There was a great all-enveloping roar that seemed to go on and on. Behind, Sergeant Smith 175 threw his hands in front of his eyes, as if he couldn't bear to watch what was going to happen.

In front of Rory the world disappeared into a scarlet, blinding maelstrom of intense light. He screamed. An excruciating pain shot through his body. Then all was darkness and he was falling . . . falling . . . falling . . .

He had come to in the Third US Field Hospital in Nancy. The surgeons had been reticent, but firm. In a quiet voice the leading surgeon had told him that they had been forced to amputate his foot. The information had shocked him. But being in a ward filled with casualties from the front in Lorraine, some with both their legs shot off, had made him pull himself together; though until he was transferred to the British General Hospital in Louvain he had spent many a tormented night, wondering why he had been chosen to become a cripple at the age of 21.

Once just before he had been transferred, the ward had filled abruptly with staff officers, all wearing polished, lacquered helmets although they were miles behind the fighting front. The wounded had stared at them in bewilderment, asking themselves what was going on.

They had soon found out. The swing doors had been opened by smartly dressed MPs, also wearing helmets, white-painted this time, to allow an ugly black and white pooch to enter. But the pooch was followed a moment later as a tall, stern figure strode in, all gleaming boots and polished brass with three outsized general's stars adorning his helmet. "Jesus H. Christ!" O'Sullivan's neighbour had exclaimed in wonder. "It's old Blood an' Guts Patton. Hope he ain't gonna slap anybody today!"

Rory laughed hollowly. Everyone in the army had heard how Patton had slapped two soldiers suffering from combat fatigue in a field hospital back in Sicily in '43. The incidents had created a scandal and had cost him his job as commander of the US Seventh Army.

But on this November day, Patton had not come to slap wounded soldiers but to commend and decorate them. With his aides dancing attendance he knelt, took off his helmet and whispered something to the first grievously wounded officer at the far end of the big ward. Then he rose and snapped his fingers impatiently. Hurriedly an aide passed the Purple Heart Medal and the Bronze Star which he pinned reverently on the man's pyjama chest.

Then he made quick progress down the ward, occasionally dabbing his eyes, as if almost overcome with emotion, while the white-coated chief of the hospital gave a brief explanation of each man's wounds. Finally he had come to Rory, who sat to attention as was customary in the British Army. "Traumatic foot amputation," the surgeon explained.

Swiftly Patton went down on his one knee and breathed a combination of expensive cigar smoke and eau-de-cologne over Rory. "You're gonna do great, captain," he said. "Just great. Got shot in the arse in the last show myself, but I recovered, as you

26

can see. In the arse," he emphasised the place of his wound and gave Rory a dingy-toothed smile. Again his fingers snapped and the two medals appeared as if by magic and were pinned on Rory's chest. "America's proud of you, son," Patton said, rising to his feet with a grunt. The strain obviously telling on him.

"This officer is an Englishman, sir," the surgeon explained, looking a little worried.

"What? What's a limey doing in *my* hospital, being awarded American medals?" Patton exploded, his thin cheeks flushing an angry red.

For a moment Rory O'Sullivan thought he would tell the choleric American general he could have them back if he wished. He wouldn't be able to wear them anyway without the permission of the King. But then the look on Patton's face told him it would probably be wiser just to keep his mouth shut, which he did.

Shaking his head angrily, Patton moved on, after glaring at the chief surgeon, who winked at Rory behind Patton's back.

That had been Rory O'Sullivan's first encounter with the American general who obviously hated all Englishmen. It wasn't going to the last . . .

Chapter Four

Rory and Miles O'Sullivan could see the great man had been shaken by his recent defeat in the General Election. But he put a brave face on it as he sat there in the weak sunshine daubing on a canvas which depicted the garden at Chartwell, Kent, in which he now sat. A servant had just offered them a drink. Now they stood sipping their drinks, while he painted, a big cigar sticking out from the side of his toothless mouth.

"Well, I don't suppose you two voted for me either. They say it was the khaki vote which lost me the election," Churchill said a little sadly.

Rory, feeling sorry for the bowed figure who had led the country to victory and who had been thrown to one side when that victory had been achieved, said: "I didn't vote at all, sir. I had too many other things to do."

At his side, Miles added, "And I'm too young, sir. I'm not yet 21."

Churchill looked up slowly like a very old man and gave them a weak smile. "Well, that's honest enough, I must say." He put his brush down on to the palette and said in a business-like tone, "It's not going to be easy since I am no longer PM. But it can – and *will* be done! I want those Huns who tortured and killed our men found and punished at all cost." He continued after dipping the end of his cigar into a large glass of brandy at his side: "We can't expect very much help from the new socialist Minister of War, but we can from some of the better chaps in the War House. They will keep in radio contact with your mission, Captain O'Sullivan and arrange that you are supplied by the British Army, though this will have to be done secretly. The new British Army of the Rhine does not take kindly to what they regard as irregulars. They want to get back to peacetime soldiering, as they call it, though I'm afraid there is going to be precious little peacetime soldiering for the British Army in the years to come."

Rory nodded his agreement. He had seen what was happening in the British Zone of Occupation in Germany. The Army was trying to re-introduce the old kind of bull of the regulars. 'If it moves, salute it, if it don't, paint it white' was the way the cynical soldiers phrased it.

"Now, the best I can get you through my own sources," Churchill went on, "is two jeeps and supply trailers. That would be sufficient for two officers and six other ranks, wouldn't it?"

"Yes sir," the two O'Sullivans replied promptly. "We'd command, one to a jeep, and we've already got six volunteers from the 1st SAS Regiment, all seasoned veterans of the campaigns in Africa, Italy, France and Germany."

"Excellent!" Churchill said approvingly, taking a hearty gulp of his brandy. "That's the kind of chap you want." But he raised his finger in warning. "But remember this – *officially* the Special Air Service no longer exists. If you are rumbled, it could mean trouble, serious trouble, for all of you, including the other ranks. It would mean a court-martial and," he shrugged, "unfortunately, I and all the others involved would have to deny any knowledge of the matter. I, in particular, for obvious political reasons."

"Yes sir, I understand fully," Rory snapped urgently. "We're prepared to take that risk."

Again he remembered the shock of finding the mutilated, tortured bodies of the two captured SAS men on that lonely road after they had ambushed the German Gestapo convoy: one with the smashed-in face; the other with a gaping wound, gory-red and horrible, where his genitals had been. The memory of that terrible discovery still haunted him and strengthened his determination to find Dr Barsch, the swine who had ordered that to be done to the unfortunate young men.

"You will be my secret hunters," Churchill was saying as Rory O'Sullivan's mind flashed back to the present. The ex-PM chuckled, "It would be one in the eye for the brasshats if they knew that the SAS still existed, even if it consisted only of eight men. You know," his eyes grew dreamy, "once I had planned that a handful of you chaps would either kidnap or kill Rommel in the summer of 1944. That would have brought the war in the West to a far speedier conclusion. It wasn't to be. But it shows what a handful of men could do." He took another drink. "But I mustn't rabbit on. Finish your drinks, gentlemen and be on your way."

They did as Churchill ordered, clicked to attention and saluted smartly.

Churchill touched his cigar to his forehead in the semblance of a salute and said, "Good hunting, gentlemen!" Then his face went blank and it seemed as if he had already forgotten them.

At the gate that led out of the garden, the two officers looked back at the great man. He was slumped unmoving on his stool, not even drinking, the cigar leaking smoke purposelessly in his pudgy hand. For all the world, Rory told himself, it seemed as if Winston Churchill was already no longer.

In the jeep on their way back to London, the two officers considered their task. "Smith 175 will go of course," Rory said thoughtfully, indicating the gigantic ex-guardsman in front driving the little open vehicle.

"We'll need an interpreter too," Miles agreed. "I've talked to Rosenblum." He meant the little German Jew who had volunteered from the Pioneer Corps to fight with the SAS. "When I grow old," Rosenblum was wont to say in that thick German accent of his, "I don't want to tell my grandkids that I spent that Big War shovelling shit in Stoke-on-Trent." Miles went on: "He's keen to come. He says he's got several scores to pay off personally. Keen as mustard!"

"Tashy Kennedy is coming," Rory said. "He says he's coming just for the beer and women."

Miles laughed. "He would – and then we need Corporal Stevens. He's our best radio operator. We need him to keep in touch with the War House."

Slowly, as they came ever closer to the much-blitzed capital, they worked out their team and then turned to weapons and supplies, with Rory saying, "Well, now the war's over we can't go driving about in the other zones of occupation looking like teams of heavily armed brigands. We can take our personal weapons. But we'll strip the jeeps of the Vickers and Browning machine-guns, hiding a couple of Bren MGs in the trailers, just in case. You never know. There is some talk of werewolves, you know."

"What are they when they're at home?" Miles O'Sullivan asked. He had heard rumours.

"Some sort of secret German resistance, made up of Nazi fanatics. They've already killed the German Mayor of Aachen and a few from other German cities because they collaborated with our people. I don't want to take any chances, especially as no one will be taking any note of our actions. We're on our own and accountable only to ourselves and Winston Churchill."

"Point taken," Miles agreed sagely. "But where are we going to start, Rory? Germany's a bloody big country and there are supposed to be about ten million refugees and German nationals wandering about all over the show. It'll be like looking for a needle in a haystack, Rory."

"Agreed, but I think we can make certain assumptions," Rory answered.

"What?"

"Well, Intelligence is pretty sure that he's not in the British Zone of Occupation. He was on our automatic arrest category list and we knew where he lived there before the war. We put a watch on his wife – a big fat *deutsche Hausfrau* type – and his relatives there. Not a sign. He's hardly likely to go underground in the French Zone of Occupation to the south of the British Zone. After four years working for the Gestapo in France there'd be a good chance that he might be recognised by someone he'd knocked about. So that leaves the US Zone of Occupation."

"Still a big area," Miles objected.

"I know, I know!"

Up at the wheel Smith hooted his horn angrily at a group of dirty-faced urchins playing in the ruins who, taking them for a Americans, were holding out their hands hopefully, crying, "Any gum, GI?"

"Bloody Yanks," Smith cursed as they sped by followed by the jeers of the kids, shouting, "They're only frigging British soldiers! They ain't got nuthin'."

Rory shook his head. "A minor thing, Miles. But it goes to show. We've come down in the world since the war started. Even our own kids make fun of us. No matter! Back to our own business. So we're left, as I said, with the US Zone of Occupation."

"Yes, I'd thought of that, too, Rory," Miles agreed. "In particular, Bavaria."

"Why Bavaria?" Rory asked, suddenly puzzled.

"On account of General Patton, commander of the US 3rd Army."

Rory remembered that scene with the medals in the hospital over half a year before. He hadn't even bothered to obtain permission to wear the two US gongs. "Oh him! But why?"

"Because what I've learned from our Intelligence wallahs is that Patton is so prejudiced against the Russians – he sees Reds under the bed everywhere – he's refusing to sack the old Nazis. He thinks we're going to need them for the next war with Russia."

"Oh my sainted aunt!" Rory groaned. "We've just ended one bloody war! But go on, Miles."

"Now, after his victories in France and Germany and especially in the Battle of the Bulge where he thinks he baled General Eisenhower out and prevented an American defeat, he feels that he's above the law. Already, it appears, Ike has criticised him because he keeps known Nazis in office in Bavaria and that

33

he is supposedly maintaining German troops under arms, including SS battalions. Patton simply takes no notice. What would you do, Rory, if you were a Nazi on the run in Occupied Germany this autumn?"

"I get you. I'd head for Bavaria on account of Patton's attitude."

"Exactly and there's more to it than that."

"What?"

"It was in the Bavarian and Austrian Alps that the Nazis were supposed to be going to make their last stand at the end of the war. They'd built fortifications there, moved in crack troops, stocked weapons, food and the like. That would be another attraction for our war criminal on the run, Rory."

"I take your point, Miles. So we start in Bavaria!"

Miles nodded his agreement, while Rory looked thoughtful as he considered the problem for a few minutes. Now they were driving through the ruined suburbs of the capital, with a few gleaming white 'prefabs', as they were called, erected recently on cleared spaces. Here and there a Union Jack hung limply from a post and there was tattered bunting draped across the street which had been put up to celebrate the VE Day street parties. Once they spotted a sign painted on a house announcing '*Welcome Home, Jack. We're Proud of You*'. Underneath it someone had scrawled hastily, '*Yes, and ask her what she was doing with them Yanks while you was away, Jack!*'

Rory looked glum. Even in victory there was an air of decay and defeat about everything. And it wasn't just combat-weariness after six years of total war. It was a malaise that went deeper than that. He dismissed the gloomy thought and told himself that he was more determined than ever to show their former enemies, who were now perhaps enjoying American protection, that the British Lion still had sharp teeth and could bite.

"Miles," he snapped with renewed energy, "I'm going to give you 48 hours to get the jeeps organised and the teams briefed. The boys can have the third day off. Then in 72 hours we sail from Dover for Calais and from there we're heading straight for Old Blood an' Guts' in Bavaria."

At the wheel, Smith 175 laughed happily and chortled, "That's the stuff to give the troops, sir! I never thought I'd be glad to get out of Blighty after all the years I've bin away. But I am now. The frigging place puts years on me." He pressed his foot down hard on the accelerator and the jeep shot forward as if Smith 175 couldn't get to Dover quickly enough.

Chapter Five

In Occupied Germany it was a time without precedent.

The beaten downtrodden or defiant German losers called it *'die Stunde Null'* – the zero hour – where time stood still and nothing seemed to being done by the victors. It was chaos without parallel. One of Europe's greatest countries, which in the early '40s had ruled an Empire bigger than that of the Romans, was now in a state of total collapse.

There was no gas or electricity, little fuel save that looted from the bomb-sites and precious little water and food. There were no railways working, no public transport, no mail. The civilian telephone lines didn't work. There were no radio broadcasts save these authorised by the victors and the conquerors ran the handful of newspapers allowed to the civilians.

New food rationing had been introduced, but there was no means of collecting and distributing that food. Of the total population of 80 million, only a handful were males and these were mainly war cripples, boys and old and feeble grandfathers. The rest of the Fatherland's male population was either dead, on the run, or behind barbed wire in cages all over the world from Africa to America.

Ten million foreigners, former slave workers and ex-POWs, wandered about the defeated, wrecked country, trying to find their way back home, living off their wits, looting, stealing, raping as they went.

Each major city in the country had been wrecked up to 70 per cent. The dead still lay unburied beneath the wreckage. In the ruins were the survivors, selling whatever they could, including their bodies, to the conquerors for cans of food and cigarettes.

VD was endemic. For ten cigarettes the average soldier, however ugly, could have a different woman every night. As for their generals and senior officers they took titled mistresses, lived in castles and ruled like medieval potentates. *Der Herr General*, regardless of whatever army he belonged to, Russian, British, American or French, was the new *Gauleiter*, expecting and demanding that his every whim and wish be catered for.

General George S. Patton was no exception. He rode and hunted. He gave exclusive receptions for his senior commanders, complete with fine wines, and food imported from the States. But at the same time, Patton, who couldn't really settle down after two years of combat, was worried about his future and Eisenhower's policy towards their erstwhile allies, the Russians, who he called privately the 'Mongolians', his thin face contorted with angry scorn.

On the same day that Rory and Miles O'Sullivan had their fateful meeting with Churchill and the two SAS officers decided that they would start their search for Dr Barsch in Bavaria, Patton was telephoned at his Bavarian headquarters at Bad Toelz by no less a person than the former Supreme Commander, General Eisenhower.

'Ike' had a complaint to make. "Georgie," he said from his HQ in Frankfurt, "the Soviet High Command has been making complaints to me about you."

"Have they?" Patton asked in apparent ignorance

37

as Willie, his ugly bull-terrier, snored at his booted feet. The dog had belonged to an English fighter pilot who had been shot down. "What complaint?"

"They say that you are too slow . . . too slow in disbanding German Army formations, even SS, in Bavaria. They want to know why, Georgie."

Patton flushed angrily.

At his feet Willie started and moved away to the other side of the big, ornate office as if he expected there was going to be trouble.

"Hell!" Patton exploded. "Why do you care what those goddam Russians think, Ike? We are going to have to fight them sooner or later. Perhaps within the next generation. Why not do it now while my Army is intact and the damn Russians can have their hind-end kicked right back into Russia in three months. I'd go through them like shit through a goose." He gasped for breath. "We can do it ourselves with the help of the German troops we have. All we have to do is to arm them and take them with us. They hate the Red bastards!"

"Shut up, Georgie, you fool!" Eisenhower shouted angrily over the phone. "This line may be tapped. You'll be starting a war with Russia with all your talk!"

Patton refused to shut up. "I'd like to see it get started some way or other. That's the best thing we can do now, Ike. *You*," he added with a note of scorn in his high-pitched voice, "don't have to get mixed up in it. If you're that damned soft about it and scared of losing your rank, let me handle it down here. In ten days I can make enough incidents happen to have us at war with the sons-of-bitches and make it look like their fault." He gasped for breath again with the effort of so much talk. "So much so that we will be completely justified in attacking them and running them out."

Eisenhower cursed and slammed down the phone.

Suddenly in high good humour, Patton stared across at his aide Colonel Codman, who had been listening to the conversation. "You heard that, Codman?"

The handsome middle-aged Bostonian, who supplied Patton with the fine French wines that he loved at his fancy receptions, nodded. "Yes sir."

"I really believe," Patton said with a smug smile at the thought of Eisenhower's discomfiture, "that we are going to fight the Mongolians. If our country doesn't do it now, we'll have to take them on in years to come when the Russians will be ready for us. Then we'll have one Sam Hill of a time whipping the red bastards. But we'll need the Germans. And I'll tell you this, Codman, we'll need the Germans. They're they only people in Western Europe who've got a bit of spunk left. The limeys are effete, worn out and now they've even got Reds governing them since they kicked that old drunk Churchill out. The Frogs are okay for food and wine, but that's about it. De Gaulle's got no control over them and most of the intellectuals and workers are commies already. As for the Italians – well, what can you expect from people who are lower than the *A*-rabs!" He contorted his face with disgust. "No, we're gonna have to rely in the Germans."

Codman remembered the times when his boss had railed at the 'Huns' and 'Krauts' and had threatened to take no German prisoners when the going had been tough for his beloved Third Army. Then the Germans had been at the "bottom of my personal shit list", as he had often snarled. Things had changed drastically, Codman told himself.

"No," Patton concluded, reaching for one of the large cigars he loved to smoke, against doctor's orders, "we simply can't go on mistreating the Germans when we will one day expect them to fight for us. Things are going to change, have got to change. And here in Bavaria I'm gonna see, Codman, that they do. Codman, when you're through here, show in my chief-of-counter-intelligence Colonel Helmut Ziller. I think it's about time I had a serious chat with our tame Kraut colonel."

Colonel Helmut had been taken from the 'old country', as he still called Germany, at the age of three and moved with his parents to a little German farming community in Nebraska. Although he had gone to grade and high school there, he still spoke English with an accent; but then at home and with his buddies he had always spoken his native German. Even when he had risen to become a sergeant in the local state police, he still spoke the language of 'ze old country' with his fellow troopers.

He was a big man, well over 6 ft tall, with blond cropped hair and light blue, wary eyes. It was said of him that he could see into a man's very soul within three seconds. Unfortunately, back in 1943 when he had been first posted to England as a member of the US Military Police, he had failed to do so when confronted with his middle-aged village policeman. At the time he had been trying to arrest a 'nigra' at pistol point for some alleged offence.

It had been then that the fat, slow-moving bobby had got off his bicycle, removed his cycle clips and said in the traditional, carefully deceptive manner used to defuse potentially explosive situations, "Now then, Yank, what's all this little lot about?" He had beamed at the big American police lieutenant, with a big Colt 45 in his ham of a fist, staring angrily at the little Negro pressed up against the pub's wall.

"This guy's refusing to be arrested," Ziller had snarled, not taking his icy glaze off the terrified black for an instant. "And, for that, he is in very serious trouble indeed." He deliberately clicked off the safety.

"What's he done, Yank?" the bobby had asked, a big smile on his homely, ruddy-cheeked face.

"Insulted a white man, that's what he's done," Ziller had answered seriously, as if that was the most heinous crime in the world. "Now then, nigger," he snapped, ignoring the British policeman in his tight uniform. "Are you gonna come along peaceful-like or are we gonna have trouble, eh?" There had been iron in his voice.

"But Cap'n, sir, I never did do nuthin'," the terrified black man had protested. "That white man he insulted me and I didn't think it was right in front of mah lady friends."

"Lady friends," Ziller had sneered. "*Where?*"

"What did he say, son?" the bobby had asked carefully.

"He done said that we black folk all had tails – like monkeys."

"Cut out the cackle!" Ziller had broken in. "Are you coming or not?" He raised his pistol. "If you're not, you're gonna be one dead nigger—"

He never finished the sentence. The middle-aged bobby had laid him out with one blow of his truncheon. It was then that the 'limeys' had become yet another of the nationalities and races that Lieutenant Colonel Helmut Ziller hated. Now Ziller, blond, big, cropped, stood rigidly to attention in front of Patton while the latter gave his 'tame Kraut' his orders.

41

"You know me, Ziller. You've been with me a year now. I want to win over the Germans, not make 'em hate our guts, as it seems some of our people, especially the kikes, do."

Kikes were another of Colonel Ziller's pet hates. He gave a stiff little bow in the fashion of his Prussian ancestors. "I understand perfectly, General Patton."

"Good, so this is what I want from you as chief-of-counter-intelligence. You will – *apparently* – continue Shaef's policy of non-fraternisation between us and the Germans." He laughed scornfully and added, "Hell, I always say a soldier who won't fuck won't fight and in my Third Army, any soldier who lays a German girl – as long as he keeps his helmet on – ain't fraternising, he's *fornicating*."* Patton laughed.

If Patton laughed, Ziller didn't. He had absolutely no sense of humour. His hard face remained as set and rigid as always. The only emotion he gave vent to was a look of impatience, as if he were willing his boss to get on with his orders so that he could carry them out as soon as possible.

Patton continued in the end with, "Naturally I want to know whether there is any attempt at conspiracy in Bavaria against my Third Army. But pay more attention to the commies than the Nazis. The latter know which side their bread's buttered on. They're with us."

Ziller nodded stiffly. 'Commies' were another of his pet hates. "I shall do that, sir."

"Good, and one other thing, Ziller. If anyone comes snooping around in Bavaria – you know, those kikes from Shaef or from the Frogs and limeys looking for war

* Eisenhower had ordered that there would no dealings with the Germans save on official business. This was called the 'non-fraternising ban'.

criminals," he said the words as if they were in italics, "I want to know. Those guys are only trouble-makers and we've got problems enough without alienating the Bavarians any further. Is that clear?"

"Yes sir," Ziller answered smartly. Patton was thinking on the very same wave-length as he was.

"One last thing, Ziller," Patton said, his smile vanished. "It's this business of the werewolves. You're in the picture of course, aren't you?"

"Sir."

"Now I regard these teenage hoodlums and gangsters in the mountains," he pointed out of the big window of his office at the snow-capped peaks of the Alps in the far distance, "or wherever they're hiding out, as dangerous to my Third Army. They're definitely anti-American and I don't want them infecting the local populace with any of their crack-pot ideas."

"Sir," Ziller answered, as wooden as ever.

"They are definitely to be eradicated wherever you find them. Is that understood?"

"Yes sir. That's quite clear."

Patton waved his hand in dismissal. "Okay, Ziller, get on the stick."

Ziller clicked to attention, saluted rigidly and went.

Patton watched him go. Then he shook his greying head, half in wonder, half in amusement.

"Willie," he said to the ugly pooch at the other side of the office. "You can take a kraut out of krautland, but you can't take the kraut out of him wherever he goddam lives." Then he forgot Ziller and, staring into the mirror opposite which he had had placed there specifically for this purpose, he started practising his 'war face number one'. He'd probably need it again once America started fighting the 'Mongolians'.

Chapter Six

Joe Rosenblum was drunk. It was something which didn't happen very often with him. On account of the terrible things that had happened in his young life since he had fled Germany in 1936, he always liked to keep a clear head. But when he went 'out on the razzle,' as the boys of the SAS called it, he always took a couple of stiff drinks. This time he had taken more than a couple, but he needed a woman – he was determined he would never touch a German woman once they returned to the defeated country and with his looks he wouldn't be very successful if he didn't push his luck. And for that he needed the boldness that drink gave him.

Now he sauntered down a darkening Shaftesbury Avenue, swaying slightly, but not over much so. Anyway he had just passed two redcaps and they hadn't even looked at him so he couldn't be so bad, he told himself.

The London street was packed with service men and women, mostly tarts, he told himself, working the poorly paid British servicemen, now that the Americans were returning in droves to their own country. There were some Americans about, including many WACs, probably employed in the capital. Joe Rosenblum eyed them tentatively. He knew that the Yank soldiers contemptuously called them, 'GIs with

44

built-in foxholes.' It was crude but that was the way they thought of the American women soldiers. Not that they seemed to be interested in the men, for all he knew they could have been lesbians.

He sniffed and wondered if he should go into a pub and have another drink. It was growing dark and he didn't want to end up with a tart for the night. There was no telling what a man might get from one of the thousands of amateur and professional whores who had been plying their trade in London throughout the war. He wouldn't be the first squaddie to get what the troops called 'a full house', both kinds of venereal disease, from some raddled whore.

Rosenblum decided against another drink and wandered on slowly, into Leicester Square searching the faces of the passing women with more boldness than he was accustomed. But in the end it wasn't Joe Rosenblum who did the finding. Instead *he* was found. Just as he turned the corner into Charing Cross Road a pleasant, slightly foreign-sounding voice asked, "You gotta a light for a lady, soldier?"

He turned startled. An American WAC master sergeant, with more medal ribbons on her delightful breast than he had after two years of combat, was standing there, flourishing a cigarette and smiling up at him winningly.

"Why of course, miss," he stuttered, "er, sergeant." Hurriedly he fumbled with his lighter while she smiled at him, obviously amused at his nervousness. He flicked the wheel. In the sudden burst of blue light he took in the dark eyes and features and recognised her immediately for what she was: a foreign-born Jew just as he was. He saw something else, too. The American woman was smart, very smart. The dark eyes were full of a

45

burning, keen intelligence, tinged, he thought, though he didn't know exactly how he knew, with a certain kind of sadness or perhaps regret.

She puffed out the first blue smoke, her eyes crinkling a little. But she didn't move on. That emboldened him. He cleared his throat, for really he was no ladies man. He left that sort of stuff to his comrades like 'Tashy' and the very handsome Corporal Stevens. "Could I invite you to a drink, er Sergeant?"

She laughed lightly and said, "Listen I know I *am* a sergeant, but I don't think a guy who I've just picked up off the street in a foreign country needs to be too formal, though I guess it's a foreign country to you, too, huh?"

He nodded.

"I guessed so! Well, why don't you just call me Lisa."

"Of course, of course," he agreed readily, amazed at his luck.

"And your name?" she prompted.

"Joe, the lads call me. But my real name is – was – Josef."

"German Jew?"

He nodded.

She reached out her hand and took his. Her grip was surprisingly firm and dry, not like his own palm which was damp with sweat at the effort of picking up a girl like this. "Frankfurt," she said. "Fled in '36."

"Munich," he answered. "*Jahrgang '36*" – a 'vintage year' as he called it.

They laughed and she said, "I've got a better idea than going into a pub for a drink. I'm on leave in London . . . I've got a 72-hour pass. I'm staying at a small hotel, with my own room and a kind of little sitting

46

room, just down the road from here. And," she lowered her voice and made herself sound very seductive in a self-mocking manner, "I've also got a quart of 'Four Roses', if you're not scared of being taken advantage of by a female Yank, sir?" She laughed.

Joe Rosenblum didn't know what 'Four Roses' was but he liked Lisa's sense of humour and even more he liked the proposition she was making him. He felt his blood quicken and a racing feeling spread through his loins. "I don't mind being taken advantage of," he said thickly.

"Well, we'll see," she said more seriously now. "I just like to talk to somebody. These kids," she indicated a group of passing WACs, "just don't know what the score is. Why should they?" She indicated the blue wings on his shoulder flash, the ribbon of the Military Medal on his chest and two gold stripes on his sleeve which indicated that he had been wounded twice. "I know the limey insignia. I can see you've been around. I'd like to talk to somebody who talks the same language as I do."

He hesitated, telling himself he had never met anyone quite like Lisa before.

She noted the hesitation and said, "You know I'm not a nice Jewish girl any more. Do you want to call it off?"

"No, of course, not," he stammered, overwhelmed by the directness of the American girl. "I'm off to Germany tomorrow—"

She didn't give him time to finish. Instead she thrust her arm under his. "Let's go!" she commanded.

So they strode down the street, arm in arm, stared at by soldiers and civilians alike. It wasn't every day that you saw an American female master sergeant propelling a somewhat worried and foreign-looking SAS trooper down the street!

They had made love greedily, at times almost angrily. They had both started off awkwardly after a couple of drinks of the Four Roses. He had fumbled and faltered as he had undressed her, as if she had been the first woman he had made love to. In the end, when he had succeeded in getting off most of her uniform, she had ripped off her own panties, gasping a little, her eyes glinting a little feverishly in the dim electric light.

She had parted her legs and revealed the line, pink and damp, in the middle of the jet-black bush of pubic hair. "There, that's what you want, isn't it?" she had hissed almost challengingly.

He had hardened immediately and had thrust himself against her soft white belly. She had moaned deep down in her throat, her eyes closed, as if she were in ecstasy, groping blindly for his organ. She had jerked it up and down in a hard, unfeeling manner, sobbing almost as if to herself, "Oh, I need it . . . God do I need it!" Then she had lapsed into Yiddish, which Joe didn't understand save for the word *"meschugge"* – "crazy".

He had thrust her backwards against the table. She went willingly. He had spread her thighs, with her sobbing and babbling in Yiddish all the time. Then he had inserted his penis into her, noting that she was as tight as a virgin. Lisa was not wanton, that was clear, even though she had made all the advances.

Thereafter it had been different. She had been tender, no longer so hectic, showering his lips with little butterfly kisses, whispering in his ear that she was going to please *him* now that he had pleased her.

48

"Anything you want, Joe. Just say and I'll do it. Even *that* – if it gives you pleasure."

"Would you?" he asked incredulously. The only time he had enjoyed that kind of sexual pleasure had been with an Arab whore back in '43 in Algiers and she had given him a dose of crabs.

"Yes," she whispered and slid her face down his body, kissing his chest, licking lightly at his nipples, then on to his hairy loins before finally taking him in her mouth that felt as hot as a fiery oven. He shivered with pleasure. Then she went to work on him, slowly and seductively, so that he had to grit his teeth to stop himself for crying out with the sheer erotic pleasure of it all.

He did not let her complete the act. Instead he rose. He turned her over and pushed her on to her back. He crouched over her like a demon, his hair wild, his dark eyes burning into hers, he thrust his strong rigid penis into her, as she held her legs spread wide above her head. Thrusting, thrusting, pounding, pounding, both of them making wild unintelligible cries, both lathered in a hot sweat, their stomachs slapping against one another, they seemed to go on for ever and ever, until she gasped in a strangled moan, as if she might well be dying "*Joe . . . Joe . . . I'm finished!*"

In that same instant, he collapsed on top of her wet, feverishly hot body, satisfied at last . . .

In the middle of the night, both lying tightly together in the single bed, smoking reflectively, with the sounds of London outside, it might have seemed that they were the last people alive in the capital, she started to talk. She did not look at him, her voice was toneless and without emotion so that it appeared that she was talking to herself, though he knew she wasn't; for this was a kind of confession.

"He was just a kid, you know. I was three years older. He was with the Ivy League, the Fourth Infantry Division. They knew they were scheduled to land on D-Day and he was scared. I was already in counter-intelligence by then and he asked me did I think there'd be a lot of opposition. Of course, I said it would be a walkover. The Germans were about finished after Russia. But it didn't help much. I knew he was still scared. He talked a lot about his folks back home, some little punk township in the Mid-West, farmers I guess, and how he'd never see them again." She stubbed out her cigarette and without looking at Joe lit another one immediately. They heard Big Ben chime four. Joe said nothing. He knew it was something that Lisa had to get off her chest; something which would explain her behaviour this night.

"So I let him do it to me, Joe. He was a *goy* but it didn't matter. Gentile or not, he was just another scared young man who thought he was going to die. It was the first time for me – and for him. It wasn't very good, I guess. But it helped him – well, I like to think it did. Then a couple of weeks later he was gone, like they were all gone. I didn't know when they were going of course. But on that June day I went over to Weymouth – we all knew the invasion convoys would group just off the place. And the sea was empty. Somebody had drawn that goddam stupid '*Kilroy wuz here*' on the wall near where I was standing. I'm not a fanciful sort of person, Joe, but then I burst into tears." She choked for a moment, but caught herself. "He was killed that day," she said baldly and without emotion, or so it appeared, "on Utah Beach and he wasn't even 19."

It was just after Big Ben had struck five in the morning – and still neither of them could find the peace of mind to go to sleep – that she started to talk again, and Joe held her hand tightly in his, thinking that the gesture might help her. "So after Ben was killed, I vowed that I'd make the Nazis pay. Before, it had been because I was Jewish and I had been hounded out of the country in which I had been born by the fascists. Now it was for Ben."

"Go on," Joe said encouragingly.

"So I routed the bastards out where I could find them. At Shaef they thought I was a very tough cookie, and I was! They used to say, 'Take it easy, Sarge. You can't take on the whole Nazi Party single-handed.' I took no notice. I had to make them pay for that poor dead Mid-Western farmboy who would never go home again." He heard the catch in her voice as she said the words and for a moment felt envious: she had really loved her 'Ben'.

"So," she went, controlling herself again, "when the Germans surrendered last May, I thought it was all over. I thought I could go back to the States and start a new life. I fancied studying acting." She gave a brittle laugh. "I know my ankles are too thick and I'm too short and I look too Jewish, but that was a fancy that took me."

He began to protest that she was a beautiful woman, but she pressed his hand hard as if telling him to stop.

"But it wasn't," she said simply, a sudden harshness in her voice.

"What do you mean?"

"Well, perhaps you've heard of these so-called werewolves, who have been killing Germans who were prepared to work with the Allies."

"Yes, a bit," he admitted.

"Well, Shaef in Frankfurt sent me to Bavaria to find out what General Patton, who's the governor there – you've heard of him? – thought."

Joe nodded cautiously. After all he had only known Lisa a matter of hours, though it seemed like years.

"Of course, I didn't get to see Old Blood an' Guts, though I did see his chief-of-counter-intelligence, a man named Colonel Helmut Ziller—"

"A German?"

"*Officially* an American, but put him in SS uniform and you couldn't tell him from one of the worst of those Nazi bastards," she said bitterly.

"And?"

"Well, this Ziller sounded off about the 'kikies' and that all Germans weren't bad and that *his* general didn't want the folk from Shaef coming poking their long noses into what was going on in Bavaria and that in the end we'd need the Krauts to fight with us against the Russians."

Joe whistled softly. "Jesus, hasn't there been enough fighting?"

She didn't seem to hear. Instead, she said, "I did a little checking on Lieutenant Colonel Helmut Ziller and I discovered he's not too *stubenrein*" – she used the old German word for 'clean' – "as he is supposed to be. Ziller, to my way of thinking, is up to something. You know that when Germany was about beaten, nearly 100 million dollars' worth of German gold was shipped to Bavaria from Berlin. I think that someone is paying Colonel Ziller some of that gold . . ."

Chapter Seven

"Fancy little Joe here getting in the pearly gates of an American master sergeant," Tashy Kennedy mocked as he held on to the collar of Stevens' tunic as he vomited over the ferry rail although they had just passed out of Dover harbour and the sea was as smooth as a mirror. "Seems a bit perverted to me." He took the Woodbine out of his mouth and said to a wretched Stevens, "You're gonna lose yer ring, mate, if you puke any more."

Stevens vomited even more.

"She ain't that kind of girl," Joe said hotly.

"They're all that kind of girl," Tashy opined. "Black, brown, white or yeller – they're all the same with their legs spread!"

"Shut up," Rory snapped without rancour, considering what the little German-Jew had learned from the American counter-intelligence agent.

Up front a group of drunken soldiers returning to the Continent were wailing, *"Now this is number one and he's got her on the run. Roll me over in the clover and do it agen . . .!"*

"What else did your – er – friend say?" he ventured.

"Well, sir, she said that the centre of anything illegal going on is in the Garmisch area."

"Didn't that use to be a ski resort or something? I remember it vaguely from before the war."

"Yes sir," Joe Rosenblum agreed. "But now it's important for the black market bigshots and Nazi crowd because it's close to Austria and Italy. They can do a quick bunk if needs be. Anyway that's what my friend said."

At the railing a miserable Stevens moaned, "Tashy, just let me frigging well die, will yer? I've never puked as much as this in my whole frigging! life."

After a moment, Rory said, "Perhaps that's where we should start, Joe."

"Well, we've got to start somewhere, sir, and my friend sez she'll keep in contact. Give us the latest gen on this Colonel Ziller bloke I've already mentioned."

"That's good," Rory said enthusiastically. "An inside contact could be very useful!"

Joe Rosenblum beamed, proud with himself and his 'contact'. "She'll come through, sir, I'm sure."

At the railing, Tashy said, "I thought you was supposed to be doing the throughing, Joe? Or do you Jewish blokes do it different than the rest of us?"

Joe Rosenblum made an obscene gesture with the two fingers of his right hand.

Tashy laughed a little wearily. "Can't help yer there, mate," he commented. "Got a double-decker bus up there already." Then he turned his attention to the handsome Corporal Stevens, saying, "Oh, come on, pack it in! You've already filled the Channel with puke and the fish are beginning to protest!"

Stevens retched on, without the slightest consideration for the fish in the Channel.

*　　*　　*

Two hours later they were on their way, rolling across a now strangely peaceful and empty France, heading east for Metz. Now the soldiers had gone, and with them the great supply depots which had fed the front. The last time they had come this way, every roadside had been piled high with crates of shells, rations and jerricans full of petrol. Now all was empty, the only sign that a war had been fought here was shattered farms and the rusting, wrecked tanks in the shell-pocked fields, each with a circle of wooden crosses around it where the dead crew had been buried till the Graves Registration people would come and dig them up again.

As they rolled across that great flat plain towards the heights of Verdun, the peasants toiling in the fields turned and stared at them curiously, as if wondering what soldiers were doing in their country once again. Now and again they were stopped by patrols of French troops, sloppy and obviously ill-disciplined, with cigarettes glued to their bottom lips as they challenged the jeeps. Rory in the lead jeep knew how to handle them. There was no talk of passes, travel documents and the like as there would have been in the British Army. Instead, a tin of 50 Capstan-ration cigarettes changed hands and they were waved on without any further questions being asked.

"What a shower o' shit!" Smith 175 commented as they passed through the last patrol by means of the usual bribe. He swerved to avoid a shell hole in the cobbled road. "Can't have squaddies looking like that."

Rory laughed softly. "We're not all ex-Guardsmen, Smithie, you know. But what do you expect from a country that was defeated by the Germans and where most people took the least line of resistance and just let the Jerries get on with it? All the same," he added more seriously, eyeing the wooded heights ahead, "We can't afford to be complacent."

"What do you mean, sir?" Smith 175 at the wheel asked.

"At the Intelligence briefing at the War House just before we left, they told me the border area between France and Germany is highly dangerous. There are armed gangs of deserters, black marketeers and former *Milice*," the armed French militia who had supported the Germans, "running stuff in and out of the French Zone of Occupation and not adverse to a little bit of highway robbery."

Smith 175 frowned threateningly. "Let' em try it on yours truly and then they'll see what'll happen to the Frog sods. I had enough of that *Milice* lot when we was operating in Alsace last autumn. I'll give 'em the old whatfor."*

"Well said, Smithie," Rory said with a grin. "I'm sure you will."

Then they rolled on in silence.

An hour later, with the light beginning to go, they started to roll through Verdun, heading for the River Meuse and the grim chalk heighs above. In the streets no one took much notice of them. Verdun had seen enough soldiers in two world wars to be concerned about yet more soldiers.

"Do you know," Rory said to Smith as they headed for the Meuse bridge, "that in the First World War more than 2,000,000 or so men fought up there on the right in an area of just ten square miles."

* See John. Kerrigan: *Surprise Attack*, for further details.

"I know, Boss," Smith answered, flashing a glance at yet another cemetery, for they seemed to be everywhere around Verdun, "I read about it. The sods should have knocked the shit out of each other then and then we'd not have had this last little lot."

Rory smiled. "History isn't, I'm afraid, that simple, Smithie." He sucked his teeth thoughtfully. "We'd better start thinking where we're going to kip for the night, before the light goes altogether."

"I was thinking the same, Boss," Smith 175 agreed. "What about a Frog whorehouse for starters?"

Rory chuckled. "You had your chance last night in the Big Smoke, Smithie."

"Well I did cock my leg over an old tart, Boss," Smith 175 admitted. "But it cost a packet."

Rory O'Sullivan ignored the comment as he stared at the white chalk height above. "Perhaps we could doss up there. I don't think there'll be too many people visiting the battlefield at this time of the night. Too many ghosts, I suppose."

Smith gave a little shudder at the thought. "'Spect you're right, Boss. So that's it."

"Yes," Rory agreed a little grimly. "That's it. That's where the greatest battle in history took place. They say on wet days the mustard gas stills rises from the hollows down there and that you can't use a compass around here because there's so much metal under the earth, tons of it still, that the needle won't stay still."

"Christ," Smith 175 cursed. "It's gonna be pleasant dreams tonight, all right."

Behind them the radio operator, Corporal Stevens, well recovered from his recent sea sickness began to sing, *"Kiss me goodnight, sar'nt major, tuck me in my little wooden bed. We all love you, sar'nt major—"* until

57

WESTERN MILITARY DISTRICT
Occupation Zones

○ U.S. 3rd Army Zone of Occupation

Smith 175 growled, "Put a frigging sock in it, Stevens, or I'll do yer!"

"You and whose frigging army?" Stevens said defiantly. All the same, he did stop singing, as if he, too, were overcome by the oppressive, doom-laden atmosphere of those grim lonely heights, where once so many thousands of young men had died in vain.

Fifteen minutes later they had turned off the climbing, winding hill road and entered the stunted shrub forest which now covered the great battlefield, trying to find a sheltered spot out of the cold wind which had commenced to blow with the fall of night. Veterans that they were they soon found a spot: a glade surrounded with trees and dotted here and there with the foxholes of another war. Tashy even found a battered, rusting Poilu's helmet, exclaiming as he did so, "Make a nice pisspot for the night!"

But no one laughed. They were much too sombre, as if even the most unimaginative of them felt the grim aura of this accursed place.

All the same they soon had their little two-man tents erected and were squatted around the blue flames of the petrol-charged tommy-cookers, frying soya-link sausages and bacon that came in a long roll from the compo ration tins, while Smith 175 passed round them, handing each man a measure of strong, brown GS rum. It was illegal, for the rum ration was only supposed to be served when men were at the front line, but as Rory O'Sullivan reasoned, "We're still fighting the war although it's over. So give the lads their firewater!" and the lads were not complaining.

While they waited for their share of the tinned sausage and bacon, washed down with a jug of strong 'sar'nt-major's char', the two officers discussed the plan

59

for the morrow when they would reach the frontier of Occupied Germany.

"I think entry through the French Zone would be the most wise," Rory said, dropping the map on to the floor of the tent for by now it was too dark to see it. "The Frogs are easily bribed, as we have already seen on the way here, and once we're in I think there'll be ample space to get from their zone to that of the Yanks."

"Agreed," Miles said, his stomach rumbling as Stevens turned the bacon and he caught a whiff of the cheap meat sizzling. "The Yanks can't cover the whole frontier between their zone and that of the Frogs. Why should they?"

"Exactly. After all, the Yanks and Frogs are supposed to be allies!"

Now it was almost night. Crouched in their tent, the two officers tucked into the bacon and sausage, telling themselves that this was like the war all over again, enjoying the simple pleasures of cheap tinned food and thick tea, enriched by a whole tin of Carnation milk. As Rory remarked, "With a bit of luck on our part, Miles, we'll be eating at the Savoy or the Connaught one day. But we'll always remember this good plain grub, and nothing will ever taste the same again."

Miles smiled fondly. "I suppose you're right, Rory." He gave a little polite belch as he finished the last of the triangular, skinless soya-link sausage. "But I suppose it's really the company, isn't it!"

Rory nodded and yawned as he put the greasy mess-tin down. "Suppose you're right. What do you think? Shall we post a sentry, Miles?"

Miles stared around at the darkness, broken only by the cherry-red glimmers of cigarette ends as the tired SAS troopers had their last cigarette of the day.

"Yes, Rory, something tells me we ought to."

Half an hour later the little camp was fast asleep, the only sound the night wind over the remote, dread heights and the occasional soft cough from the sentry, crouched in a century-old shell-hole, his company the battered skeleton of some long dead young man.

Chapter Eight

It was just after three in the morning and it was decidedly chill as Joe Rosenblum took over for his hour on duty from Tashy Kennedy, crouching straightaway in the shell-hole in order to escape the wind. Tashy Kennedy had shaken the skeleton's bony claw, whispering, "Ta, ta mate" and adding for Joe's benefit, "He ain't much of a talker, Joe. Not much in the way of company at all."

Joe had hissed an obscenity and Tashy had gone back to his tent, laughing softly at what he thought was his great sense of humour. Now Joe crouched there, staring at the sickle moon, cold and unfeeling, as it scudded in and out of the clouds. Back in 1916 his father had been wounded with a Swabian infantry regiment on these very same heights and once when he had been a little boy and German Jews had been allowed to travel freely, his father had taken him to see where he had been wounded. But now he had long forgotten where it had been. He had almost forgotten his father, in fact. God knows where he was. The last he had heard of the old man he had been taken away by a couple of Gestapo men. He supposed he was long dead like the rest.

He let his mind wander for a while, trying to kill the long hour in front of him and he had always thought that the longest stage of all was the hour between three and four in the morning. Then, time seemed to stand still and the hands of his watch hardly appeared to move.

He thought of the war and saw again the ghosts of his comrades who had fallen in battle. He thought of the girl and what she would do when she was finished with the army. Like him she would never go back to Germany. "Yes," a little voice at the back of his mind asked sharply, "and what are you going to do Josef Rosenblum? You can't stay in the army for ever. Besides, once this bloody business with Herr Doktor Barsch is cleared up, the SAS will really be wound up and there'll be no place for you in the Regular Army?"

Suddenly a slight noise to his right broke into his reverie. He was tense and alert instantly. Was it an animal? There were enough woods around on these lonely chalk-heights to support deer. It looked good terrain for rabbits and hare. God only knew there were holes enough in the chalk for them to burrow into. But instinct told him this was a two-legged animal.

Carefully, trying to make the least possible noise, he tried the old SAS trick of sniffing the air and filtering it through his nostrils as slowly as possible in an attempt to detect any familiar smell or scent.

"Yes, there it is!" the little voice at the back of his head rapsed urgently. There it definitely was. No mistaking that pungent odour of cheap French cigarettes. Whoever was out there had been recently smoking a *Gaulloise or Caporal*. But who was the hidden French watcher?

Joe Rosenblum considered for a moment. He asked himself, who'd want to be out here on these remote

63

heights in the middle of a cold night? He remembered vaguely that there had been ruined, abandoned villages up here from the time he had visited Verdun with his father all those years before. Would those wrecked ruins be housing tramps and the like? Was it possible? But what would folks like that live off?

The answer came to him in a flash. They'd be the border runners, the crooks taking black market goods in and out of Occupied Germany. Up here would be an ideal hiding place for them. He doubted if many gendarmes would venture here at night. With the border only miles away, this would be an ideal location for them. But why were they interested in the SAS's little camp? There wouldn't be many spoils to be gained here, a few weapons and several crates of Compo rations. Perhaps the jeeps? He didn't know exactly. What he did know, however, was that he had to alert the others, for already he could hear soft footfalls in the scraggy trees all around the camp. There were plenty of others out there.

Noiselessly, Joe Rosenblum clicked off the safety on his Sten gun. He levered himself out of the shell-hole and crouching low, so that he made the smallest possible silhouette in the silver darkness of the sickle moon, he started to move backwards, not taking his eyes off the trees for a moment.

He reached the officers' tent safely. Crouched at the entrance, he reached in and placed his hand over Rory O'Sullivan's mouth. "Sir," he hissed, "it's me, Joe Rosenblum."

Rory started out of his sleep. Then, realising that it was Joe and that the little trooper was using standard operating procedure to waken him when there was danger about, he moved the hand gently to make the other person aware of the fact that he knew something was the matter. "What is it, Joe? Where's the fire?"

Swiftly and in a whisper, Joe told him.

Rory O'Sullivan was awake and businesslike immediately. Using the same procedure as Joe had done, he roused Miles and put him in the picture.

Hastily the two officers buckled on their Colts, while, at a crouch, Joe sped to the other three pup tents to rouse the others.

"What's the drill, Rory?" Miles hissed urgently, as he tucked spare magazines into his waist belt adding a .36 grenade as an afterthought.

"Don't exactly know, Miles," Rory answered, doing the same with the professional ease of a soldier who had known plenty of night emergencies like this. "My first instinct is to do what old Paddy always maintained, 'Shoot and scoot'. But France is at peace. You can't go around shooting innocent Frogs – if there is such a creature. All the same we've got to be prepared for the worst. We're not going to get caught with our knickers down. We're all too long in tooth for that, old son." He finished his preparations and hissed, "Come on, let's go and have a look-see."

Now spread out evenly, hardly daring to breathe, the little group of veterans moved outside the ring of tents which was their camp, leaving Tashy Kennedy to look after the jeeps – just in case. Each man was wrapped in a cocoon of his own fears and apprehensions, but they were all confident of their ability to master any crisis that might come their way. All the same, they were puzzled by these unseen, mysterious strangers who had encircled their camp at the dead of night – and it was certain that the little camp was surrounded. They could hear the slight noises and footfalls coming from the trees on all sides.

Crouched low in the centre of the little formation, Rory waited till the moon slid behind a cloud. He made a parting gesture with both hands. His veterans understood the signal. They dived to right and left, leaving the centre of the camp empty. Rory then took standard operating procedure a little further. He looked up. The sickle moon was still hidden by a cloud, but it was beginning to glow a faint silver. That meant the moon would reappear in a few seconds. He hesitated no longer. He raised his Colt into the air and fired a single shot.

Almost immediately firing broke out and men came blundering out of the trees firing as they did so. In that same instant the moon reappeared. They were outlined by its stark silver light, a sharp, clear black. Now the SAS veterans went into action.

They aimed low. Bullets zipped through the trees. Twigs fell in a furious green rain. A man went down clutching his head and screaming shrilly. Crouching behind the jeeps, Sten gun at the ready, Joe Rosenblum cursed with surprise. The man had screamed and yelled for help in German!

The other SAS troopers were too busy firing to note that strange event. Another one of the civilians slammed to the ground and lay still.

Miles tugged out the cotter-pin of the .36 grenade. "Shall I, Rory?" he yelled above the angry snap-and-crackle of the fire fight.

"Yes!" Rory yelled back. "In for a penny, in for a pound!"

Miles hesitated no longer. He grunted and flung the grenade to his right. It exploded in a viscous burst of cherry-red angry flame. Shrapnel hissed lethally through air. Two civilians went down, groaning piteously as they did so while a third just stood there swaying and moaning and clutching his arm which was hanging on solely by a strand of gory-red flesh.

That did it. The sudden response had taken the heart out of their unknown attackers. They started to stream back through the trees occasionally turning to fire unaimed shots. But their targets, the SAS veterans, clung tightly to the ground. They weren't chancing being hit now by a stray shot.

Then it was over, the only sound the noise of battle echoing and re-echoing through those scruffy woods which had seen so much fighting, and the moan of a grievously wounded man lying in the trees somewhere or other, and the word the man kept repeating was not in French. It was in German. "*Sanitater*," the man moaned. "*Hilfe . . . Sanitater . . . bitte!*"

Crouched next to the precious jeeps Joe Rosenblum felt the small hairs at the back of his neck stand erect. *Why was someone asking for a stretcher-bearer in German in the middle of a French wood?* . . .

It was dawn now. They had struck camp immediately after the attack and set off downhill into the Plain of Woeuvre, heading for the little railway township of Etain some 15 or so miles away. As Rory had reasoned: "The camp's blown. The buggers might be back and if they don't come, we might get the law up here as soon as it's light. After all the Verdun battlefield is France's premier national monument and someone will have reported the shooting up here by now to the boys in blue."

Just before Etain they halted and pulled over into some fields, dotted with old cement bunkers and a trenchline, almost silted up. It was obviously part of the frontline in 1916. But they had no eyes for the relics of the old war, they were more concerned with their prisoner, who was strapped to a trailer. He was in a bad way. There was a large, gaping wound in his chest through which they could see the ugly grey lungs heaving to and fro in a mess of red gore. Indeed every time the prisoner coughed, blood seeped from the side of his mouth. He was already unconscious and all of them had seen enough dying men, with that typically white pinched nose they always had. He wouldn't live much longer.

"Well, Joe, what do you make of him?" Rory asked, as the others gathered, munching the hard ration biscuits which were their breakfast and taking sips at their water-bottles. They weren't cruel men or brutalised, but most of them had seen enough sudden violent death in these last years to take it all in their stride.

"Well, look at this for the start, sir," Joe said. He pulled up the dying man's sleeve and turning the arm pointed to the underside of the brawny upper arm. "You know what that is, don't you, Boss." He indicated the tattoo mark there. "Obviously someone tried to burn it out with a heated spoon, but they didn't do a very good job. You can see the tattoo mark all right."

Rory nodded grimly. "The SS blood group. They all had it marked on their arms as soon as they joined the *Waffen SS*. But he could have been in the French SS, the Dutch, the Belgian. I mean every bloody country in Europe supplied regiments to the SS when Hitler's Germany was winning. The French even formed a whole division."

"Not this chap, Boss," Joe said steadfastly. "He was a right old Jerry. I couldn't mistake that accent. Straight from Hamburg's waterfront – the red light district."

"Okay, I'll buy it," Rory said, his face set in a look of bewilderment. He asked himself what was an ex-SS man doing here in this part of French Lorraine?

"There are two other things, Boss," Joe went on, as the German started to writhe, foaming at the mouth, in what they all knew were his death throes.

"What's that?"

"There's another tattoo on his right hand. Look, Boss."

"Another?"

"Yes, here at the base of his forefinger and thumb." Expertly, Joe Rosenblum pulled the dying man's two fingers apart. "Can you see?"

Rory could. "It looks like a . . . box . . . with an extended piece to each end." He looked at the little Jew. "What do you make of it?"

Rosenblum shrugged in the Continental fashion. "Search me, Boss. Never seen anything like it before."

Rory flashed a glance at his nephew. The latter shook his head. "Clueless, old bean," he said in a flippant manner which belied his fundamental seriousness.

"And the other thing?" Rory asked sharply, as an ancient *gazogene*, a coal-gas-powered police car, rattled by heading for the grim heights of the old battlefield. They stared at it, all of them knowing why. Someone had reported the shooting during the night and had found the bodies.

They waited till the police car had gone before Rory repeated his question.

Joe Rosenblum licked his suddenly dry lips and

answered. "Do you remember the American – er lady friend of mine, Boss?"

Rory nodded. "Yes. What about it?" He looked impatient.

"You recall the American colonel she mentioned, this Colonel Ziller, the one who's a nasty piece of work?"

"Yes, yes, get on with it, Joe! You're rabbiting on like an old biddy."

Rosenblum flushed a little at the reproof. "Well, Boss," he declared. "That bloke mentioned the same American colonel."

"*What?*"

"I swear that was the name he mentioned – Helmut Ziller. Who could forget a Jerry name like that for a Yankee colonel?"

"Agreed . . . agreed. But what did he say, Joe? What connection does the Yank have with this little lot?"

"That twat went and did the unconscious thing on me when I tried to find out."

Rory's mind raced. "Well, get to it now. Find out what he can—"

He stopped short. On the trailer, the ex-SS man with the mysterious tattoo had stopped gasping for breath. He'd never breathe again.

Rory looked at Joe. "Well, I don't think we're going to find out much more there, do you?"

Joe Rosemblum shook his head.

Half an hour later they had buried the dead SS man under a hedgerow and were heading for the heights in the distance, which marked France's frontier with Occupied Germany. The stage was set, the actors were in place, the drama could commence . . .

70

PART TWO

The Secret Hunters

Chapter One

Alois Barschle, once known as Dr Anton Barsch, was a happy man. Now as he strode down the village street in his leather shorts and green-grey loden jacket, the peasant women curtsied to him and the farmers, puffing away at their great curved pipes raised their hats, complete with *federbusch*, as a sign of respect. After all he was the village schoolmaster, third in importance in these Bavarian villages to the local priest, the burgomaster or the head of the little local council.

The village had welcomed him two months before with open arms when the footsore stranger with the battered old army rucksack on his shoulders had explained that he was a schoolmaster, or had been before he had been called up for what he called jokingly the 'stubblehoppers', the infantry. The fact that he had declared himself a devout Catholic had been another point in his favour.

Apparently the previous village schoolmaster had been a fervent Nazi and fought a constant battle with Deacon Gurgl, the local priest, all the time he had been in the village until he had fled before the advancing Americans. Indeed the fact that he, Barschle, had gone down on one knee in front of everybody and asked the ancient deacon for a blessing 'for a poor weary

73

soldier' who had lost everything in the war, including his family, somewhere in the Ruhr, had clinched the deal. He had been given the post of village schoolmaster there and then.

The villagers had gone out of their way, despite the typical insularity of Bavarian villagers, to make him welcome. He had been given a room in Widow Schmitz's half-timbered house just off the village square, and the buxom widow in her late 30s, whose husband had been killed on the Russian front, had outdone herself on his behalf. Food wasn't short in the countryside – everyone slaughtered animals illegally in the middle of the night – and she fed him great pigs' knuckles, sauerkraut and piles of mashed potatoes, swimming in real country butter and milk, so that sometimes on a Sunday when she waited discreetly for him up in her bedroom, with the big crucifix above the matrimonial bed, he could hardly stagger up the stairs.

Besides, despite the boring work of trying to drum the 3 R's into the thick shaven skulls of the peasant children, who still came to school barefoot to save precious shoe leather, there was Gerda. Widow Schmitz's blonde daughter.

Even when he was humping the fat widow, his mind more often than not was on the slim charms of the 13-year-old girl with her little breasts jiggling up and down bra-less beneath her white blouse, and those long shapely legs that seemed to go on for ever. How careless she was when she lounged on the sofa beneath the usual cheap reproduction of the 'Last Supper', which seemed to adorn the kitchen of every house in the remote village. More than once she had spread her knees with the innocence of childhood and he had caught a delightful glimpse

74

of the tight white panties she wore, so skimpy, so revealing.

Once he had even managed to watch her on a Friday night as she had taken a bath in the tin tub in front of the great green tiled oven which dominated the kitchen and had nearly choked with desire at the sight of that slim naked body. That night he had sneaked into Widow Schmitz's bedroom after Gerda had gone to sleep and really rattled her bones for her until she had moaned and groaned with ecstasy; but all the time his fevered imagination had been on that slim naked body with the patch of fuzz on the spot which he swore would be his one day.

No, Barschle told himself, as he walked across to the village's one inn, the ancient *Zum Weissen Rossl*, where he would take his mid-morning cup of ersatz coffee and eat the big meat sandwhich which Widow Schmitz had prepared for him so lovingly, things had gone swimmingly for him since he had taken his 'dive' at the end of the war with his faked papers.

His past life was behind him. The prospects here were good, for a while at least. Once Germany had come through the present bad period of Occupation – and there was already talk that the Ami governor of Bavaria, a general named Patton, was seeking a confrontation with the Russians – then he could move on to better things and resume his role as a *Herr Doktor*, one who had studied at the University of Gottingen, *with honours!*

The inn, dark and smelling of stale beer and ancient lecheries, was virtually empty. At the *Stammtisch*, their regular table, a couple of pensioners were playing *skat*, slapping their cards without the energy of younger players. In the corner beneath the dusty antlers of some long-dead stag, a farmer was chopping up his bread into squares on his board and eating it with slices of salt bacon. Behind the zinc-covered bar, the owner, Herr Gustl, looked up from polishing the glasses and smiled winningly. *"Gruss Gott, Herr Lehrer!"*

At the mention of 'Mr Teacher', the other three rose to their feet and repeated the greeting *"Gross Gott, Herr Lehrer!"*

Barsch smiled, though his eyes remained cold behind the pince-nez he affected, dating back to the times when his boss *Reichsfuhrer SS* Heinrich Himmler, now dead, also affected similar glasses. In the darkness of the corner, however, next to the stove, the stranger remained seated with his head bent over his stein of beer. Barsch frowned but then dismissed the man as the innkeeper brought over his steaming cup of coffee, whispering as he bent over to serve it, "None of your ersatz muck, *Herr Lehrer*. Real bean coffee brought from an Ami on the black market in Garmisch." He smiled and added, "Hope little Franzl will do well at the end of the month?" He meant his son, who was exceedingly dumb.

"Yes, yes," Barsch said, breathing in the aroma of real coffee for the first time in months, it almost seemed years, "Franz is making very satisfactory progress indeed, *Herr Wirt*."

The innkeeper's smile grew even broader as he wished Barsch, *"Guten Appetit,"* and shuffled in his battered old carpet slippers back to his bar.

For a few minutes Barsch busied himself with his big sandwich and the delightful coffee. But slowly he was overcome by a growing sense of unease. He didn't know why exactly, but he felt it was somehow connected with the presence of the stranger. For strangers were rare

76

in these Bavarian mountain villages where everything centered on agriculture. Besides, strangers, especially in uniform, always spelled danger. He noted that when the stranger ordered another beer he spoke in accent-free Bavarian-German. He wasn't an *Ami* at least.

Time passed, the minutes of his life being ticked away by the heavy old clock in the corner with metallic inexorablity. Not that Barsch minded; he was too busy enjoying his food and drink. Besides, his mind was once again on Gerda, his landlady's daughter. That morning, when he had bent over her shoulder to help her with her arithmetic, his nostrils had been filled with the sweet scent of her young body and he had caught a tantalising glimpse of her pink-tipped child's breasts down the V-line of her blouse. It had taken all his willpower not to fondle them there and then, but he had managed to control himself.

"*Herr Barsch . . . Herr Doktor Barsch.*" The mention of his real name cut into him like a razor-sharp knife.

He looked up startled out of his wits. None of the others had heard; the stranger had spoken so softly, purposefully so, he assumed. The man didn't want to give him away.

He looked at the stranger's dark, sinister features, the eyes hidden by a pair of dark ski glasses. "No . . . no!" he stuttered hastily. "That's not my name. My name is Barschle–Alois Barschle."

The stranger looked at him contemptuously. Then he sat down without being asked and clicked his fingers at the bored innkeeper behind the bar. "*Noch ein Maas,*" he ordered. "And bring a schnapps for the *Herr Lehrer.* I don't think he's feeling too well."

"*Jawohl. Sofort der Herr,*" the innkeeper answered

swiftly for even in the dim, dust-heavy light of the inn he could see the village teacher had gone very pale indeed.

The stranger waited till the innkeeper had fussed with their drinks, wiping the scrubbed wooden table clean as if it were very important before he spoke. "You don't remember me?" he said softly.

Barsch shook his head, his mind reeling, a sick sensation at the base of his stomach.

"I thought so. *Oberssharfuhrer* Klar – clear as schnapps we used to say in those days in Metz in '42." He raised his pot mug of beer. "*Prost.*"

Barsch's heart skipped a beat. He remembered instantly where he had been in Metz in 1942. In the Lorraine's city '*Seep Dietrich Kaserne*', named after the Bavarian commander of the 'Adolf Hitler Bodyguard Division'.

It had been his job to roust out communist sympa-thisers – and there were a lot of them in the big industrial city – using the reserve battalion of the 'Bodyguard Division' as muscle. He put down his half-eaten sandwich, his appetite completely vanished.

"You must be confusing me with someone else," he stammered. "I was in Russia in '42."

The man in the dark glasses laughed cynically. "Listen, *Herr Doktor*, I've not got air in my teeth. I remember you well. Every Saturday night in the knocking shops in the Rue Gambetta with the battalion commander. Oh, yes, I remember that all right!"

Barsch tried boldness. "What do you want?" he demanded. "Don't you know all our Nazis have been dealt with by the De-Nazification Committee to which I happen to belong."

"You would, wouldn't you. Opportunists like you are

always quick on their feet. A regular Miss Twinkletoes aren't we?"

Barsch wished he dare show anger at the big ex-SS sergeant's cheek, but he daren't. He was too scared. The man had obviously sought him out for something, but for what? He didn't appear to be in the pay of American Intelligence as so many ex-Gestapo agents and SS snoopers were these days. But who did he work for?

"Would you sit down?" he asked a little weakly, all boldness fled now. "We don't want to make a scene, do we?"

Smirking, the big man with the dark glasses looked around the nearly empty taproom. "No, I don't suppose we do." He sat and for a moment he dabbed at the thin pink fluid which was beginning to dribble down his cheek from beneath the dark glass over his right eye.

Barsch wondered what the fluid could be, but made no comment. Instead he waited for the other man to speak.

The big man took his time, as if he were still making up his mind how to tackle Barsch. The heavy silence made the latter nervous. He wriggled on the hard wooden seat and looked pointedly at his wrist-watch a couple of times, as if he was in a hurry.

The big man laughed softly. "Those little yokels at the school won't miss you, *Herr Doktor*, unless you've got one of those little girls you used to like feeling up waiting for you to put your paw up her skirt."

Barsch's weak face flushed red. "How dare you make accusations like that?" he said hotly.

"I dare say anything," the other man commented harshly. "We know *all* about you, even about that little girl in Strasbourg last year before you took a dive, while some of us continued to fight for Folk, Fatherland and Führer till the bitter end." As if to emphasise his words, he removed his ski glasses for a moment.

Barsch gasped. Where his right eye had once been there was a pink, suppurating hole from which the noxious-smelling fluid trickled down on to his scarred cheek. "There you are, *Herr Doktor*. Hungary half a year ago with the Sixth SS Panzer Army. That's what the grateful Fatherland left me with," he added bitterly, "while you were taking your dive."

"I'm sorry, very sorry," Barsch said thickly, feeling a little sick. "I don't—"

The big man waved for him to be quiet and put on his dark glasses once more. "No matter. It's history now. Let me talk of why I've come here to see you."

Barsch tensed, his sickness gone as he became aware once more of the danger he might be in. "I'm just an ordinary village schoolmaster, minding his own business—" he began.

The big man cut him short brutally. "You are a wanted war criminal, Barsch," he said firmly.

Barsch flashed an anxious look about him, but none of the yokels seemed to have noticed and the innkeeper had vanished into the room behind the bar.

"The French are after you and I have information that the British might be too. All it takes is a quiet word to the authorities and you'll find yourself up to your hooter in shit, Barsch, remember that."

"Yes, yes, I will," Barsch stuttered hurriedly, now thoroughly frightened. "What is it you want from me?"

"Nothing as yet," the other man replied. "But my chief wants to see you and *he* might want something from you in connection with France."

80

"Your chief?"

"No names, no pack drill," the big man answered sharply. "He'll tell you what he wants to tell you. That's all you need to know." He jabbed a big thumb like a hairy white Bavarian sausage at his brawny chest. "I'm just a messenger boy." He chuckled, as if the words amused him, then rose to his feet, the pink fluid coursing down his cheek once more. "Take the local train to Garmisch on Saturday afternoon. You'll be met at Garmisch Station."

"But—"

"There are no buts. And if you're thinking of taking another dive, *mein lieber Herr Doktor*, forget it." He slapped the pocket of his jacket significantly, and a thoroughly alarmed Barsch could hear metal being struck. The man was carrying a pistol though the possession of a firearm by a German this year could well bring a death sentence at an Allied Military Court. The big man grinned evilly. "Garmisch, two-thirty," he said. He touched his heavy felt hat. *"Wiedersehen, Herr Doktor* . . . and don't forget to keep your hands away from underneath little girls' skirts." Then he was gone, leaving Barsch sweating heavily and in a state of total panic.

Chapter Two

GIs were everywhere in the ruins, eyeing the giggling German girls passing by slowly in pairs, occasionally raising themselves from their typical lounging position against a wall to give the women a wolf whistle, followed by, *Schokolade "Du schlafen with me, frowlein? . . ."* Then they would flash a bar of Hershey chocolate in the girls' direction, but at the same time keeping a weather eye open for the 'white mice', the US military policemen, with their white-painted helmets and white clubs.

"Thank God for the frigging navy," Tashy Kennedy said contemptuously and spat over the side of the jeep as they waited from Rosenblum to come back. "What a shower o' shit!"

"They didn't do so bad, yer know," Smith 175 said from behind the wheel of the first jeep. "This little lot is what's left over for Occupation duties. The blokes who did the fighting have gone home long ago."

"Suppose you're right, Sarge," Tashy answered without much interest.

Opposite, in a doorway, a GI was trying to buy a wrist-watch from a one-legged German in a shabby *Wehrmacht* uniform, offering a can of coffee. Deeper in the shadow, a GI was standing with his flies open while a German woman masturbated him.

82

Watching, Miles shook his head in mock sorrow. "It's like this all over Germany, Rory. The Germans are at their wits end and occupying armies are going downhill rapidly. They say the VD rate is horrific."

"Can't say I have much pity for the Huns after what they did in the war," the other officer commented. "But I admit it can't go on like this, Miles. We're all going down the drain pretty rapidly and if it isn't stopped the ones who will gain in the end will be the Russkis."

Miles nodded.

Opposite, the crippled German soldier was weeping as he handed over his watch for what appeared to be a pound tin of ration coffee. His watch was probably the last thing of any value that he possessed. Now he would starve.

"Sir!" It was Joe, looking flushed and happy in a guilty sort of way, as he came running from behind the IG Farben Building which was Eisenhower's Headquarters in Frankfurt. There Joe had met his 'lady friend', as he always called her, in the car park to the rear.

Miles forgot the weeping German, now limping away clutching his precious can of coffee, the tears still rolling down his skinny cheeks. "Rory, here comes our hero! He looks happy."

"Hope he hasn't done anything naughty with his, er, 'lady friend'?" Rory commented cheerfully.

Hastily, Joe Rosenblum told him what he had learned from the female counter-intelligence agent. It wasn't that much, yet it was significant enough to indicate what they should do next. "Garmisch is the place after all, gentlemen," Rosenblum panted. "She's sure of that. She says there are lots of loose ends, but the strands she has managed to unravel seem to indicate this."

83

He wiped his mouth and Rory said, "Take your time, Joe. Don't give yourself a heart attack."

"Thanks, Boss!" He sucked in a deep breath and continued, staring at the white-painted sign on the house opposite reading 'SOLDIERS WISE DON'T FRATERNISE!', under which some GI had scribbled, 'That don't mean me, buddy.'

"This US Colonel Ziller is somehow connected with the 'Spider'."

"The Spider, what the devil's that?" Miles queried.

"She says, Boss, she doesn't know exactly. But she thinks that it's an organisation funded with Nazi gold to get Germans on the run out of the country. She *does* know that the Spider is connected with the Werewolves. They provide the armed muscle."

Rory O'Sullivan, impressed, whistled softly. "This is getting very tricky and your lady friend thinks the whole shoot is being run from Garmisch?"

"Well, that's where Ziller has set up his headquarters and Ziller's the bloke who's providing protection for these Jerries."

Rory considered for a moment. "It's a long way from Frankfurt to Garmisch. I don't think we can make it on our jerricans."

Joe Rosenblum smiled. "Wouldn't worry about it for half a mo, sir. You know what they say about us Jewboys – we're all spivs. There must be something in it. Look at this!" As if by magic he produced from within his blouse a large buff envelope, announcing proudly, "An American trip ticket signed by a colonel in supply – perfectly legit. And as many 'gas coupons', as we Yanks say, *petrol* to you, sir, as we need. Courtesy the good old US-of-A." His American accent was woefully lacking, but at that

84

moment Joe Rosenblum could do no wrong. He was the hero of the hour.

Minutes later they were on their way, threading their way through the ruins of Frankfurt with Tashy Kennedy whistling at the girls and Corporal Stevens in the back lustily singing, *"We're off to see the wizard . . . the wonderful wizard of Oz . . .!"*

Their progress was slow. Time and time again they had to leave the *autobahn* to Munich and find their way the best they could along farm tracks running parallel to the motorway. Over and over again they came to signs stating *'Bridge down . . . detour'*, and they were forced to wander through remote villages and hamlets trying to get back to the *autobahn*. Several times they forded rivers on Bailey bridges, put up by the fighting troops the previous summer, double-tracked affairs that wallowed frighteningly on rubber pontoons up and down on the wavelets.

The roads, what was left of them, were filled with people: people of foot, people on bikes, people driving old nags, people pulling soap boxes on wheels, people pushing antiquated prams made of wicker work – the whole of Germany seemed to be on the move.

There were American Army convoys everywhere, following the signs, including those on billboards, American style, in curious rhyming couplets: 'BRING IN YOUR JEEP, WE NEVER SLEEP', at 'DON'T BE A SAP, PULL IN AND NAP', 'SAVE WEAR AND TEAR – LET'S CHECK YOUR AIR'. But there was one sign which caught their attention and made them stop for a few minutes. It read: 'DEATH AFTER DARK – MARK'. They stared at the sign curiously, wondering what exactly it signified until Corporal Stevens, who had the keenest eyesight of them all, spotted the 'mark' at the bottom of the sign and exclaimed, "Hey, look at that, people!"

"Look at what?" Rory O'Sullivan asked, puzzled.

"Down at the left-hand corner of the sign, Boss . . . It's the same mark we saw on that dead Jerry's hand in France."

Rory whistled softly. "You're right, Corp."

The handsome young corporal was right. There it was, identical to the strange tattoo on the dead German's hand. Was the sign a warning against whatever that mark recommended?

In the end they gave up trying to interpret the warning and the strange sign, but as the shadows started to lengthen and the traffic began to slacken, both German and American, on the roads, the whole party seemed seized by a kind of brooding apprehension. More than once each of them flung a glance behind as if they suspected they were being followed and Rory felt himself groping for his pistol holster as if he needed assurance that the big Colt was still there.

About seven that evening, when the countryside was bathed in complete darkness save where here and there a lantern gleamed in some lonely rural cottage window, their headlights illuminated a sign, the first of many bearing the same legend, 'YOU ARE NOW ENTERING 3RD ARMY TERRITORY. TRAFFIC LAWS STRICTLY IN FORCE.'

Miles grinned. "General Blood an' Guts Patton is making us feel very much at home, Rory, what," he commented as they rolled on.

"Well, the Yank General is supposed to be a stickler on discipline. They say during the war he made even the men in the frontline wear ties."

"Oh my sainted aunt!" Miles exclaimed. "Did they have finger bowls as well?"

Rory smiled. "Not exactly," he said, as they passed yet another sign with its stern warning a hundred yards on. Then he dismissed the autocratic general and wondered where he should bed the men down for the night. Thanks to Joe Rosenblum they had the all-important papers which would authorise them to stay at an American Army installation. But he didn't want that if he could avoid it. Someone might start asking awkward questions; what were British servicemen, with the winged dagger badge on their maroon berets, doing deep in the heart of Bavaria?

In the end he decided that they'd find some village or hamlet where they could obtain water and the like and simply take over the village hall or schoolhouse for the night. It was definitely getting too cold to camp out in their flimsy tents. The wind now was blowing straight from the snow-capped alps and he judged there'd be a frost, before morning.

Half hour later, after making a detour from the bomb-holed *autobahn* once again, they drove down a country lane which led them straight into a small, half-timbered village, with the usual carved balconies of the Lower Bavarian farmhouse, complete with huge manure heaps in front of the kitchen windows. As Joe Rosenblum had commented about them earlier, "The bigger the shit heap in front of the kitchen, the richer you are. Shows you've got more cows. It's one way to attract unattached women." To which Tashy Kennedy had replied, "No wonder the Jerries travelled half-way across Europe fighting other people. They just wanted to get away from the stink of shit, mate."

Now Rory O'Sullivan decided they had had enough;

they had been riding on the hard unyielding jeep seats all day. The time had come to stop and find a billet for the night. "Joe," he said as they braked in the tiny village square, devoid of human life save for the flickering yellow light of a petroleum lantern in the window of a big farmhouse opposite.

"Boss?"

"Get your skates on and see if you can get us somewhere to kip for the night. Bribe 'em with a tin of compo fags, something like that. Be nice if they can warm up some grub as well."

Joe Rosenblum winked. "For a tin of fags, sir, the Jerries'd sell their own grandmothers. See what I can do, Boss."

Five minutes later he was back, grinning all over his sallow face. "We've struck it lucky, sir," he said excitedly.

"How do you mean, Joe?" a weary Rory asked and yawned lazily.

"I thought it was a farmhouse. But it ain't, it's a lot better—"

"What is it, then, Joe?" Miles demanded. "Come on you little bugger, piss or get off the pot!"

"It's a home for fallen women, Boss," Joe exclaimed happily, "and there's a bleeding lot of them in there and they all look eager to do some more falling. They've been evacuated from Munich and there is only one nun in charge, and she's 80, deaf as a post and already in her virginal bed—" the rest of his explanation was interrupted by giggles and cries of "yoho!", as girls came streaming out excitedly, plump bodies outlined in the square of yellow light from the open door.

Tashy Kennedy's eyes lit up at the sight. He crossed himself with mock piety and intoned gravely, "Please

88

forgive me Lord Eisenhower, for I am now about to commit the mortal sin of fraternisation." Thereupon they stormed in the place, whooping like drunken Indians.

In the shadows the civilian who had been watching their arrival frowned, then, after picking up the cigarette-end which Tashy had thrown away in his haste to get into the home for fallen women, he decided he'd better report the arrival of these strange soldiers, who were definitely not the usual *Amis* . . .

Chapter Three

Colonel Ziller looked down at the woman they had provided him with this time. Her hand was small and delicate. Against it his erect organ seemed enormous. That pleased him; gave him a feeling of power and dominance. Between his spread legs the woman puffed and gasped. Obviously he was taking longer than she had the stamina to masturbate him. Probably she was weak from lack of food like most of these Garmisch women who were not prepared to go to bed with the victors for food. But that had been his proviso. They were to provide a woman to play with him twice a week, but she had to be examined to show she wasn't suffering from VD and she had not, under any circumstance to be a whore, amateur or professional. Naturally the organisation always respected his wishes. It *had* to – or else.

Between his legs the woman, a true blonde, touched his testicles as at the same time, she pulled his penis up and down, tiny beads of sweat gathering at the nape of her neck like opaque pearls. She was firm, but gentle, which he liked. But somehow he couldn't relax sufficiently to enjoy the experience totally.

This was probably due to the telephone call he had received from one of his sub-agents just before the woman had arrived. One of the sub-agent's local contacts had reported the presence of a handful of British soldiers in some god-forsaken village 50 miles or so from Garmisch. Neither knew what to make of them. Ziller didn't either for that matter. All the same, British troops deep in the heart of 3rd Army country was disconcerting. He wondered what was going on.

"Are you all right, sir?" the woman panted. She was very pale and there were dark circles beneath her eyes as if she might be anaemic.

"Yes, yes," he snapped, wishing she hadn't spoken. That put him off even more. "But it's not working." He decided to take a risk, knowing that the organisation's doctor had examined her only an hour before. "You must take it in your mouth. That's the only way, woman!"

The woman's bottom lip trembled as if she might be about to cry. "But that's a perversion, sir. The priests say so. Besides I've never done it before."

"Then it's about time you learned," Ziller said severely. "Besides, I'm taking a risk, too, you might be infected."

She ceased her pulling. "I'm a decent woman," she said. "I have no social diseases."

"I'm sure you are right," Ziller answered. "But a man in my position has to be careful. I want no scandal. Please proceed if you will."

She looked up a little helplessly and then down at his rampant organ, red and engorged, as if she didn't know quite what to do. He saw the look and commanded, "Just take it in your mouth and suck. That's all. I don't think that should be be too difficult for you, do you?"

She didn't answer. Instead, knowing what the organisation would give in the way of food for this

91

gross act would keep her and her baby daughter for a week or two, she took the penis tentatively into her mouth, holding the testicles firmly in both hands in the hope that this would end the whole unpleasant business more quickly. It was a long time now since Hans, her husband, missing back in 1942 at Stalingrad, had taken her but she had vague memories of what men liked in bed.

Ziller gave a little sigh, trying to forget the risk he was running with the woman. He only allowed himself real sexual intercourse once a month, with the women the organisation provided, after he had seen the woman's medical report *personally*. He was taking no chances. "One moment," he commanded, as she bent down reluctantly, her lips parted.

She stopped, the relief obvious on her face.

He wriggled and found the contraceptives he always carried with him, for even in his love life, Colonel Ziller was totally disciplined. Hastily he undid one from his gold-paper wrapper and thrust it on his penis, checking as he did so that it was sitting perfectly, leaving no skin exposed. "All right," he ordered, "you can commence now."

The woman sighed. Obediently she bent her head and started to suck him.

Now that he was sure he was safe he felt himself relax. He closed his eyes and began to enjoy the sensation.

Five minutes later, it was all over. He was satisfied. He gave the woman, who was looking very pale and sick, the cigarettes and waited for her to put on her hat and coat and go. She finished dressing and said shyly, "Shall I come again. I . . . I could learn to do it properly, sir, if you would like it." She averted her eyes, ashamed. "I'm certain I could."

He shook his head firmly. "No thank you."

"Wasn't I good enough?" she asked humbly.

"No, it's not that. It's just that I need a new woman each time . . . *a clean* woman," he emphasised. "He looked at his watch pointedly." "You'd better be off. It's 2.30 hours. There's only half an hour to curfew time and the MPS here in Garmisch are very keen. You'll spend the night in jail if they catch you out after curfew."

"Thank you, sir. Good-night, sir."

He didn't respond. She gave a little curtsey and went. He didn't look up. Already he had forgotten her, his needs were satisfied for the next couple of days. Outside, Garmisch was settling down for the night. A cold wind was blowing from the mountains and he was glad that the house he had personally requisitioned for himself had central heating instead of the usual tiled stove customary in that area. The villa was nice and snug and his five servants who were clearing up for the night went about their duties quietly. They knew they wouldn't find a better position than this in the whole of the one-time ski-and-pleasure resort. The only sound was the steady tread of the two MP sentries outside, as they paced the gravel paths. Ziller had insisted on having them. The Town Major and the middle-aged American could hardly dare refuse him. Ziller had records on everybody and he knew that the Town Major was keeping a mistress half his age in his own villa while he had a wife and four children in the States. No, the Town Mayor, like everyone else of any importance in Garmisch, was definitely in his pocket.

He forgot the guards and the Town Mayor. He started to concentrate on these English soldiers who

93

had had turned so unexpectedly in Bavaria. Somehow or other they had dodged the checks that were kept on everyone coming from the French Zone of Occupation into the Third Army area. Otherwise he would have heard of them earlier. So that meant they had entered Third Army territory illegally.

Ziller frowned at his austere reflection in the mirror opposite. It had once belonged to Adolf Hitler, one of his German cronies had told him. Indeed the chair in which he sat had been used by the Führer. It was something that made him very proud, though he kept the knowledge to himself.

He sucked his front teeth and wondered how he should proceed with these limey strangers. Should he wait till they called in at some US installation for rations and gas and then have them arrested? Or should he attempt to get rid of them in a much more drastic manner?

It took some time to make up his mind, but in the end he did so. He picked up the phone and dialled the number. Apart from the American-appointed burgomaster he was the only German in the whole place to possess a phone. It was illegal, of course, but Ziller had managed like he managed everything 'with thorough Prussian energy' as he always used to boast to himself, knowing that he came from Prussian stock which had always prided themselves on their efficiency even when they had been penniless and forced to emigrate to that racial melting-pot, America, in order to find work.

"Yes?" the voice at the other end snapped almost immediately as if the German had been waiting all along for this particular call. Unlike the German custom, the speaker didn't identify himself by his name.

Nor did Ziller. "A problem," he snapped drily. He

94

explained swiftly about the unknown English soldiers, adding when he was finished, "I think we need to look into it, don't you?"

There was a moment's pause at the other end and for once Ziller was not angry at the delay. This particular German was too powerful even for him. So he waited for the other man's decision. Outside there was no sound save that of the wind and the steady tread of the MPs. Ziller drummed his fingers on the table impatiently, but he kept his temper.

Finally the other man broke the heavy brooding silence. He said, formulating his words slowly, as if he were thinking about them very carefully, "I think the matter should be investigated. You know who they are don't you?"

Ziller was puzzled. "No," he answered.

"From the description of the cap badge they wear, we are talking about the special English force called the SAS."

"Like you SS?"

"No, no, these men are parachutists. They operated behind our lines in the West during the war. The Führer ordered them shot out of hand, whether they were in uniform or not. He felt they were so dangerous."

"I see," Ziller said, though he didn't.

"So, they present a danger to our great operation." He paused significantly and then said, "Will we be covered by your people?"

"Of course," Ziller agreed eagerly. "They are here in the Third Army area illegally. Officially I know nothing of them."

"*Schon gut*," the German at the other end said, his voice silky, but full of menace. "That makes it easier, I think."

"What—" Ziller began. But it was to no purpose. There was a metallic click and the phone went dead.

At the other end of Garmisch, beneath the overhanging mountain shelf, the 'Blind One', as he was known to the hierarchy of the 'Spider', stroked his grey tabby cat with his long, lacquered nails, and it purred with contentment. Dieter, his boy, had placed one of his favourite records on the phonograph and while he thought he half-listened to the words, which he supposed were forbidden now by those *Ami* swine:

> *"I have surrendered myself*
> *With hand and heart*
> *To you, my German Fatherland."*

If he had been capable of weeping, he would now. Every time he heard the words they made him feel as if he must cry. He steeled himself and considered what should be done. Things were going smoothly and Ziller was a great help. But he harboured no illusions, the longer they let the operation run, the more likely it would be blown, there were too many people involved. Most were German patriots, but there were time-servers, too, in it for the money and the goodies.

Now these English had turned up from nowhere. Did that mean that the English Secret Service, which everyone knew was very devious and cunning, were on to them?

The music ceased and Dieter, always so attentive and loving, came across, kissed him on the lips and said, "Something different, Uncle?"

'*Der Blinde*' shook his head and chuckled softly.

96

"No, I feel like more of the same – something suitably noble and patriotic. One more time. I've just decided to have someone killed." He chuckled again and this time the sound was decidedly unpleasant . . .

Chapter Four

"Cor ferk a duck!" Tashy Kennedy commented happily as they moved lazily to the waiting jeeps, followed by the waves of the 'fallen women', who had for the most part 'fallen' again during the night. "That really took the lead out of my bleeding pencil!"

"Well," Stevens said a little sourly, "I hope they didn't give yer anything in the way of a souvenir!"

"Don't put the frigging mokkers on it!" the other man said.

Up in the lead jeep studying the map, trying to work out the best route to Garmisch, Rory O'Sullivan shook his head. "Soldiers," he said, as if the word itself was significant. "Ruddy soldiers!"

Miles smiled. "It's a rough old life, Rory. They've got to have some pleasure!"

"I suppose so," his uncle agreed, "so long as it doesn't entail a course of penicillin shots in the bum."

"Amen to that," his nephew said and then the two of them concentrated on the pre-war map, which of course didn't show all the detours and the like which now plagued anyone travelling the *autobahn* to the Bavarian alps.

In the shadows, the shabby civilian watched them, as he had been ordered to do. He didn't know why, but it didn't do to get on the wrong side of the 'Spider'. People

98

who did, both German and *Amis*, found themselves in trouble. Bodies of murdered people were being found floating down the River Isar almost daily and there were sinister rumours circulating throughout Bavaria about the power of the underground organisation. Some said the Party would be back in power in a couple of years, supported this time by the *Amis*, who would need Germans to fight their war for them against the Ivans. Everyone knew that the Americans were no soldiers. Only the Germans knew how to fight and beat – the Russians.

Rory made his decision. The 50-mile or so journey to Garmisch would take them most of the morning if the conditions were as they had been the previous day. The sooner they started the better.

He nodded to Smith 175. "All right, Smithie, let's get them out of this house before they shag themselves to death. You think they hadn't ever seen a woman before. They carried on like schoolboys!"

Smith 175 grinned a little wearily. He, too, had had his share of the 'fallen women' during the night. "It wasn't the boys, sir," he replied. "It was the Judies. They couldn't get enough of it. It's been weeks, perhaps months, for most of them since they had a bit of the other. That old nun must have watched them like a frigging hawk." He waved to the old crone in the dirty black habit who was watching them from an upper window, as if she were wondering where these strange happy men had come from.

Smith 175 waved to her happily. "Ta, ta, old stick! Wish we could have stayed a bit longer. Might have given yer some more infants to look after."

Automatically the nun waved back and Rory

O'Sullivan said, amused by it all, "Come on, Smithie. You've said your goodbyes, let's move it!"

"Yes Boss." Smith let out the clutch and the jeep, followed by the other one, started to roll down the cobbled village street stained here and there by the yellow droppings of the oxen which the peasants used to pull their carts to and fro from their fields. Behind them the women waved frantically and one of them was openly crying. Tashy Kennedy shook his head fondly. "She's in love with me, you know," he said to Stevens. "It's allus like that with me and the Judies. Once I've been up their knickers they're no use to any other man." He looked down at his dirty nails in mock modesty. "You know how I'm built down there, don't yer!"

Stevens shook his head, and made no comment.

As the two jeeps cleared the village, still followed by the cheering of the 'fallen women' and the blubbing of the woman who Tashy had 'pleasured', as he liked to put it, the watcher quickened his pace. It was necessary, he knew, to report immediately. The organisation was very keen on efficiency . . .

They rode southwards most of that day. They were delayed time and time again by the signs they had first encountered the day before: 'ROAD OUT' . . . 'BRIDGE BLOWN' . . . and invariably 'DETOUR!' As Smith 175 commented with a sigh, "The whole of ruddy Germany seems to be one great frigging detour".

"You can say that again," Miles O'Sullivan agreed, shifting a little wearily in his seat as he eyed another crowd of wretched, ragged Germans and ex-soldiers, clambering down into the hole beneath the wrecked bridge and up the other side, each person obviously out for himself, too weary or underfed to help the mothers attempting to get their children in those strange basket-like prams of theirs through.

At two Rory called a halt so that the men could 'brew up'. He picked an isolated spot because he was sick of the barefoot children with legs like bean-shoots who came begging for sweets and cigarettes every time they stopped. Groaning and stretching their stiff bones the men set about cooking 'sar'nt-major's char' over the spluttering, flaring, petrol-fuelled tommy cookers. Others began to open compo ration tins with their jackknives.

Five minutes later they were squatting under the trees, spooning 'Meat and Vegetable' stew out of their square ration tins and gratefully sipping scalding hot, dark-brown tea.

Miles and Rory studied the map yet again. They estimated they were still ten or 15 miles east of Garmisch, but as Rory said, "This time I think we'll do it before nightfall and we'll go to the nearest Yank installation for grub and petrol. I know it's a bit risky if people start asking awkward questions, but Joe wants to get in touch with his lady friend in Frankfurt. He thinks she might have some more info for us now."

Miles nodded his understanding and then frowned, a little puzzled.

Rory saw the look and asked swiftly, "A penny for them, Miles?"

"Over there," Miles answered. "At three o'clock. There's a tank, a US Sherman by the look of the silhouette."

Rory squinted against the low rays of the autumn sun and stared at the black shape which had cleared the breast of the hill some half a mile away and had commenced rolling towards them. He sniffed. "Funny, what's a lone Yankee tank doing out here in the middle of nowhere?"

"Exactly. Don't they know the war's over and Hitler's long dead?" Miles smiled.

Rory O'Sullivan, his uncle, didn't smile. There was something about the Sherman, all battened down as if this was wartime, so there was no sign of the tank commander. That was slightly sinister. He didn't know why, but he was suddenly overcome by a sensation of unease.

"What do you think, Miles?" he asked, as one by one the men stopped eating to stare at the lone tank bearing down upon them out of nowhere.

"Bit strange," the other officer said. "Look," he added, a note of sudden alarm in his voice.

The barrel of the 76mm gun on the tank was beginning to swing from side to side like the snout of some predatory monster attempting to sniff out its prey.

"Eh!" Smith 175 shouted in sudden apprehension. "What's yon Yankee sod think he's up—" He never finished his shout.

There was an abrupt crack, followed by a loud, searing noise like a piece of canvas being ripped apart.

Whump! To their immediate front a brown, steaming hole appeared abruptly like the work of some monstrous mole. Shrapnel, hot and silver-glowing, sliced the air lethally. "Fuck this for a game of soldiers" Tashy Kennedy yelled. "The bugger's shooting at us!"

The Sherman was. As the driver rumbled to a halt, the gunner in his turret fired once more. Another shell hissed menacingly through the still, afternoon air.

Hastily the SAS troopers, veterans that they were,

dived for cover. The shell exploded only yards away from where they were eating. In a heal of upturned messtins and spilled tea, they lay there as the earth quaked and trembled beneath them.

The Sherman's engines roared again. Certain of victory, the Sherman was beginning to roll again, heading straight for where they lay. In minutes, they knew the tank's rubber-shod tracks would be crushing them if they didn't do something.

Corporal Stevens acted. He sprang to his feet, Sten-gun in hand. It was David and Goliath: a lone human figure against the massive 30-ton tank, but the handsome young blond corporal knew what he was doing. He would attempt to rattle the tank's gunner and driver while the others attempted to knock the metal monster out. Now he started to fire controlled bursts against the tank's frontal apertures, relying on his keen eyesight – and luck.

Stevens' bursts did the trick. The gunner fired again, but this time the shell was well out of range, howling over their heads to explode yards behind them.

"Keep it up, Corp!" Rory O'Sullivan yelled and sprang to his feet. Next instant he was hobbling quite fast, for a man with one foot, into the dead ground to the right of the Sherman, already tugging at the grenade in his pocket.

Stevens ducked as the turret gunner fired his co-axial machine-gun, the tracer heading for him in a lethal white stream. Then he rose a second later and ripped off another burst. Slugs howled off the turret armour like heavy tropical rain on a tin roof. He ducked once more, knowing that his luck was beginning to run out; knowing that the officer would already be working his way to the rear of the slow-moving Sherman.

103

Lying prone with the rest, Miles shouted, "Start firing . . . Rattle the buggers! Come on now – *FIRE*!" He pulled out his own Colt and, knowing his bullets would have absolutely no effect on the Sherman's thick metal hide, fired at it all the same. The rest joined in.

Now Rory O'Sullivan was some 12 yards behind the Sherman. He could see the glow of the tank's exhaust quite clearly and felt the gravel and soil flung up by the flailing rubber-tracks. He quickened his pace, knowing that there was no chance of anyone seeing him in the tank, as long as the crew kept the turret buttoned down.

It was only a yard away now. He tugged the pin out of the .36 grenade, wondering how he should stop the 30-ton monster. If he knocked off one of the tank's tracks to bring the Sherman to a halt, the crew inside were virtually impregnable and they could still continue to use their superior armament. It would have to be the exhaust. That might well set the Sherman alight and the American tank was notorious for the way it caught fire so easily. Indeed its crews cynically called it 'the Ronson', after the famous cigarette-lighter because of that weakness.

He felt the heat of the exhaust sear his hand. It was now or never. He flung the grenade, fell to the ground and rolled over all in one and the same moment. There was a thick crump. For a moment nothing much seemed to happen. Then the Sherman erupted into violent, angry purple fire. The flames seared its deck like a giant blowtorch.

Hurriedly Rory O'Sullivan rolled farther down the hill to get away from that deadly, all-consuming flame, his uniform already beginning to smoulder.

Inside, the Sherman was racked by a series of muffled thumps as its ammunition began to explode. Rory sheltered his face with his arm, blinking and gasping in the intense heat. It wouldn't be long now. If the crew didn't bale out soon they never would.

The Sherman braked to a halt. Another muffled explosion. Then the turret was flung open. A mushroom of white smoke rose from the open turret. Now he could hear the screams of agony and yells of fear. A hand, already charred and skeletal, appeared. With terrible, agonising slowness, the air around it stinking of burnt flesh, it heaved and the dying man appeared, blue flames wreathing his body, tearing greedily at him. He slumped over the turret rim and tumbled slowly to the ground, dead before he reached it.

Below, the driver opened his escape hatch. Rory tensed, Colt at the ready. The driver in his little, lower compartment might well have been more protected from the flame. He had. A little man, trousers on fire dropped to the ground, turning and writhing madly as he tried to put out the flames which threatened to engulf him.

At the top of his voice, Rory yelled frantically, "Run, man . . . run! She'll go up in a minute. *RUN FOR YOUR LIFE!*"

Somehow or other, gasping with fear, the lone survivor staggered to where Rory lay full length in the grass, waiting for the inevitable to come. Hastily Rory slapped out the flames with his beret and then tensed, face pressed to the earth.

The inevitable happened. Suddenly the Sherman heaved and trembled crazily. Blue flames shot out from the open turret. There was a rending of metal. Tracer ammunition zig-zagged crazily into the afternoon sky.

With a great, ponderous roar that seemed to go on for ever, the turret rose from the chassis, rolling slowly over, and then with increasing speed slammed into the ground some 20 feet away. The Sherman from the unknown was dead.

Chapter Five

The little man with the charred face and blisters running up his right arm looked at Joe Rosenblum sullenly. Fifty yards away the Sherman was still burning, the paint crackling and bubbling in the intense heat like the symptoms of some loathsome skin disease.

At first they had thought he was an American, dressed for some inexplicable reason in civilian clothes, but when they had tried to question him, he had shrugged and murmured, '*Nix verstehen.*' The little man was obviously a German.

That realisation had shocked the SAS troopers. They looked at each other in bewilderment and Smith 175 had expressed all their thoughts when he asked, "How does a Jerry come to be driving a sodding Yankee tank, eh?"

So far they had received no answer to that overwhelming question. But after Miles had patched him up the best he could from what they had in the jeep's medical chest and they had given the little man a cigarette to soothe his shattered nerves, they were determined to get some answers. First the attack in Northern France; now this. It seemed to all of them that someone had it in for them.

Joe Rosenblum had interrogated plenty of prisoners in the past year and as he always said, "It's no use going at it like a bull at a gate. Softly . . . softly . . . the old sweet and sour treatment, that's the way to get results, especially with the Jerries."

So he started off with a fairly harmless question, asking, "How come you know how to drive an *Ami* Sherman tank?"

The little man shrugged again and said, "I was with the Skorzeny Brigade back in December '44. Some of us learned to drive them for the Ardennes attack."

Swiftly Rosenblum interpreted the man's words, adding, "You remember, sir? Skorzeny – the bloke who rescued Mussolini – and then led a brigade wearing Yankee uniforms during the Battle of the Bulge?"

Rory nodded and Miles said, "This bloke is obviously used to clandestine ops."

"Yes," his uncle said. "Okay, Joe, get on with it. I don't want to hang about here too long if I can help it. You never know . . ." He didn't complete the sentence, but his listeners knew what he meant. There could be more trouble on the way.

"Where did the tank come from?" Joe Rosenblum asked quietly. Still he desisted from posing the direct questions which might cause problems. His aim was to lull the prisoner into a sense of false calm. Then he'd go at him on the whys and wherefores.

"Fifty-Sixth US Ordnance Depot, *Gebirgsjager-kaserne*, Mittenwald," the little man answered.

"I see. Were the others *Amis*?" Joe asked, indicating the charred corpse half hanging out of the burnt turret. He was giving the little man a chance to say they were and clear himself as perhaps a civilian driver working for the Yanks. That would give him a line to go on.

Surprisingly, the little German didn't fall for it.

"No," he answered tonelessly. "They were from the old Skorzeny Brigade, like me."

Joe pounced. "So how did you get the Sherman? After all you were all Germans, weren't you and the *Amis* are not in a habit of giving their tanks to their recent enemies, I would think." He looked hard at the little man.

Again he shrugged almost carelessly. "We had orders," he answered woodenly.

"*Orders*. From whom?"

"An *Ami*."

Swiftly Joe translated for the benefit of the others and Rory, leaning forward eagerly, snapped, "Ask him what kind of, er, *Ami*." He used the German word.

The little man looked at Joe Rosenblum. "I don't know. I didn't take the order. But an *Ami* who got us the order to take it for a test run."

"Test run?"

"Yes, that was the excuse to get it out of the *Kaserne*."

Joe whistled softly at the information. "An officer?"

Again the little man shrugged almost carelessly. He was great at shrugging. "Could be. I don't know."

Joe controlled himself with difficulty, but he knew it was futile to lose his temper. He took out a packet of Woodbines. "Here," he said, with a fake smile. "Have a lung torpedo."

The man accepted the cigarette almost as if it was his right. Joe leaned forward and lit it with the treasured Zippo lighter that the American woman, Lisa, had given him as a parting present.

"*Danke!*"

"What can you tell me?" he persisted, as the

little man breathed the blue smoke out gratefully.

"Not much," he began, but Joe Rosenblum decided the time had come to change his tactics from 'sweet' to 'sour'.

He reached forward and grabbed the little man by the front of his charred jacket. "Don't lark around with me," he snapped. "One more crappy remark like that and I'll have the eggs off'n you with a blunt razor blade."

The little man blanched as the cigarette fell from his mouth and dropped to the ground. "What did I do wrong?" he panted. "I'm—"

"Don't shit me!" Joe cried, working himself up to that artificial rage which he knew intimidated POWs, especially after they had been treated gently at the beginning. "Look at my face. What do you see, bastard German: I'll tell you," he cried bringing his face closer to that of the suddenly terrified little man. "I'm a Yid, Kike, Hebrew, *messugge* Jew. I hate you Nazis! I could snuff you out without blinking an eyelid, without a second thought after what you lot have done to my people. Do you understand that, arse without ears?"

"Yes, yes," the little man agreed eagerly. "I understand, sir."

"All right, then, let's have no more frigging around. I'm going to ask you more questions and I want answers – no more frigging double talk." As if to emphasise that he meant business, very serious business, Joe Rosenblum took out his Colt, cocked it slowly and laid the heavy pistol on his right knee with his hand resting on it. It looked as if he might use the weapon at any moment.

The little man gulped.

110

"All right," Joe Rosenblum went on, taking a deep breath like a man who was controlling himself with some difficulty. "Who's this *Ami* officer who got you the order to take the Sherman out of the *Kaserne*?"

"I don't know, sir," the little man answered desperately. "Honest I don't. All I know is that he's a big shot."

"Did you see him?" Joe rasped.

"Not this time. But I've seen him one time before in Garmisch."

"You'd recognise him if you ever saw him again?" Rosenblum looked significantly at Rory and Miles.

"Yes . . . yes sir, I think I would."

"Good!" Joe Rosenblum lowered his voice making it less strident now, as if he were pleased with the little man's responses. "Do you think it was this *Ami* officer who gave the order to have us killed, because that's what you were going to do, wasn't it – *kill us*?"

The little man lowered his gaze and said in a toneless manner, "Yes, I suppose so."

Joe Rosenblum changed his tack. "Well, who are – were – you lot anyway?"

The little man hesitated. Then as if the mark explained everything, he extended his right hand to reveal the tattoo between his thumb and forefinger.

Rosenblum whistled softly and Rory O'Sullivan said, "The same mark as the bloke in France."

"Yes sir," the interpreter agreed. "Well, what does it mean?" he shot the question at the little man.

"It's the sign of the werewolf, sir," was the answer.

"But in what three devils' names have the werewolves got to do with us and an *Ami*—" He broke off suddenly, as the little man's hand shot and grabbed the pistol resting on his knee.

The sudden move caught Rosenblum – all of them – completely off his guard. Now the little man's hangdog look turned to one of triumph. "All right, Jewboy," he snapped. "Now the boots on the other foot isn't it." He reached forward and slapped the muzzle of the heavy pistol across Rosenblum's surprised face. Joe yelled with pain and reeled back.

The little man got to his feet, his dark eyes searching the faces of the SAS troopers all around him. "One of you move," he hissed in German, "and the Jewboy gets it!"

Most of them didn't speak much German, but the way he pointed the pistol at Rosenblum's heart told them all they wanted to know. He was going to kill Joe if they made a wrong move.

"Hold it there," Rory commanded as the little man started to back off towards the first of their jeeps. He knew what the German was about. He was going to take the jeep and drive away with it. But he couldn't be allowed to do that. They couldn't afford to be without that jeep in the wilds of Bavaria. Besides, the little man was the only lead they had to whatever was going on here. There might be a connection to *Herr Doktor* Barsch, the reason they had come here in the first place. The little man *had* to be stopped.

Rory's mind raced desperately. The little man was almost level with the jeep now. In a second he'd be inside it and starting up the motor and Rory guessed he'd fire a couple of shots into the engine of the second jeep to immobilise it and prevent them from following him.

Suddenly Rory had it. It was an old trick, but it just might work. "Ready," he hissed through his clenched teeth and then raising his voice and looking over the little man's right shoulder, he called, "*Get him, Peter!*"

Instinctively the little man flashed a glance to his rear to find that there was no one there. *"Du Schwein!"* he screamed, turning to his front once more.

But already it was too late. Stevens was up on his feet in a flash and raced forward. The little man raised his pistol but Stevens dived forward like a professional scrumhalf. The little man went reeling back, but he kept the pistol tight in his right hand. Rory could see the sudden whiteness of the knuckle of his trigger finger as the two of them rolled round and round, Stevens trying to get the Colt from him. In a moment the little German would fire.

A muffled shot rang out. Rory cursed as the fight ceased immediately. For what seemed an age the two of them lay there, still and unmoving, like two spent lovers. Then Rory gave a sigh of relief. Stevens staggered to his feet and peered down at the little man who lay there in the extravagant posture of those done violently to death. Stevens peered down at him for an instant, then he tugged the Colt from suddenly nerveless fingers to reveal the scorch mark, flecked with the cherry red of blood on the little man's front. He shook his head. They knew what that meant, they had lost their key informant. The little German was dead . . .

Chapter Six

Frau Schmitz heaved and panted as Barsch thrust himself in and out of her. He was not experiencing much pleasure in the bedding of the heavily built widow but she expected it of him, and in the end it would lead to what he really desired – *Gerda*!

Now she was gasping, eyes pressed tightly closed, moaning, "More . . . oh, please, more . . . *PLEASE!*"

He hissed, "Not so loud, *Liebchen*. We don't want the child to hear, do we!"

Barsch was sure they were making enough noise in their love-making to be heard across the road at the inn – and after all a village schoolmaster had to be discreet, especially in Catholic Bavaria.

Peering through the keyhole, Gerda watched fascinated as her mother rose and fell, carrying the bespectacled teacher up and down with her. It was funny but at the same time exciting, though she didn't quite know how to get some relief from the itch between her skinny little legs from the sight.

On the big matrimonial bed, with the Apostles staring down from their 'Last Supper' as if they had suddenly lost their appetites, the Widow Schmitz writhed and tossed in the last throes of her ecstasy. "*Ich spende,*" she moaned. Her face contorted and her head turned to one side in a strangled gasp, as if she were dying.

"Oh my God!" muttered Barsch and pulled himself out of the woman rapidly. That was the last thing he wanted: to have an illegimate child with the stupid peasant woman. He had worries enough already.

Frau Schmitz gave one last sigh, then fell back on the sheet, one hand falling over her face, her huge breasts slumping to each side of her torso, the breath coming from her lungs as if from a cracked bellows. "Oh, *Herr Lehrer*," she said throatily, tears beginning to course down her fat, doughy face. "How kind and good you are to me! What have I done to deserve someone like you, an educated man too!"

At the keyhole Gerda stopped playing with herself. Feeling a little cheated that her mother had some sort of experience, she didn't know exactly what, while she hadn't, she muttered, "Silly cow! Why couldn't she have kept doing it till something happened—"

She stopped short. In the mirror in the dark hall below she could see the reflection of a face peering in through the glass part of the door. She pulled her hand out of her knickers as if it were suddenly red-hot and dropped the black skirt that she had once worn when she had been a member of the Hitler Youth, feeling her face flush. She hoped he hadn't seen her, whoever he was. Then she reasoned he couldn't have.

Inside the bedroom, Widow Schmitz was still shedding grateful tears, muttering her thanks and how she would "dearly love to bear your child, *Herr Lehrer*", a sentiment which sent shivers up and down Barsch's spine as he pulled on his trousers, whispering to the fat *Hausfrau*, "Now you rest, dear Mrs Schmitz. You deserve it. You have done so much for me."

"Have I, dear teacher?" she sobbed happily and raising her ample buttocks she drew on the black

115

silk knickers, dating back to her honeymoon so many years before, which she always put on for these 'special occasions', as she called their weekly love-making.

Politely Barsch kissed her work-worn hand and said, "I shall go below and get on with my marking. I've got a whole set of books with *'schonschreiben'** to go through for Monday. *Adieu!*"

"*Adieu mein Kavalier!*" she simpered. "How gallant you are!"

He closed the bedroom door behind him and heard her begin to snore even before he was half-way down the creaking wooden stairs.

"*Onkel!*" The voice startled him.

He turned. It was beautiful little Gerda lurking there in the shadows. He looked down at her somewhat crestfallen face. "Anything the matter my treasure?" he asked, hoping that he had already done up his flies on the stairs.

She pouted. "Yes, *Onkel*. You're always with *Mutti*. You never seem to have any time for me – like at the beginning." She looked up at him and if Barsch had been a wise man, which he wasn't, he would have realised there and then that he was being lured into a trap. "Why can't you spoil me like you do *Mutti*?"

"Spoil her?" he queried stupidly. "I don't quite understand. But perhaps as your possible future stepfather you and I should have a little heart-to-heart talk, Gerda." Taking her hand and, fighting off an almost overwhelming inclination to grab those pre-pubescent breasts of hers, he led her to the couch in what the peasants called 'the best room', used normally on

---

* Literally 'beautiful writing'. Something in the nature of a copper-plate hand.

Sundays and high feast days. She let herself be led willing and now for the first time he smelled the slightly fishy odour of sex coming from her. There was no mistaking it. He told himself she had not cleaned herself thoroughly after coming from the earth privy next to the pigsty. These peasants, he knew, were not too careful with their personal hygiene.

He sat down carefully on the overstuffed sofa and she plumped herself happily next to him, her thin legs spread so that he got an even stronger whiff of the sex odour. Above them Frau Schmitz snored heavily so that the lamp trembled quite violently.

"Now then, my little darling," he said winningly like a good uncle should, "what's the problem?"

She pouted. "I don't know how to say it, Uncle," she began.

"Straight from the liver, my little darling," he said, using the peasant expression and, taking a chance, pressed her right knee. "You know I'm always here for you, especially *you*," and he pressed her knee even harder. She didn't seem to object.

"Well," she continued. "I'm jealous."

"*Jealous*?"

"Yes," she answered, pouting her thick underlip even more. "Why can't you do the things you do to *Mutti* to me too?"

"Things?" he asked, his heart racing now, but knowing at the same time he was on dangerous ground. After all, she wasn't even 14 yet. "What kind of things?"

"Well, you know. Things that make *Mutti* moan and groan, and make her cry and send her to sleep even though it's very early." She indicated above her where *Mutti* was still snoring loudly.

117

His mind flashed back to that dramatic night in Strasbourg last year before he had fled across the Rhine to Germany and prepared to go underground. He had got the teenage girl drunk. He had been scared but at the same time too sexually aroused to worry about the consequences. He had taken her on the office couch brutally and violently. She had screamed and struggled, but he knew instinctively that her screams were spurious. She had *enjoyed* having it thrust into her with such force.

Afterwards she had not cried. Instead she had lain there in the red gloom, moaning softly as if he had hurt her physically. After a while he had had put his hand carefully between her skinny, girlish legs. The crevice had been wet and hot. He knew that she had been wanting it again. How corrupt and degenerate she had been, despite the fact that she had worn the uniform of the Hitler Maidens.

The thought had aroused him once again. He had felt himself grow erect at the thought of her shamelessness. He had thrown himself upon her skinny-ribbed body. She had wimpered and wriggled furiously as he had pumped himself savagely into her. "Now you bitch," he had gasped, his pince-nez steaming up with the effort, "now you're getting what you've been crying out for all the time, aren't you. Speak up!" And he had slapped her almost angrily across the face.

That had started her. She had seemed to go mad with lust. Savagely she had sunk her teeth into his naked chest, then had mouthed vile obscenities, learned God knows where. And then suddenly she had arched her spine wildly so that for one dreadful moment he had been afraid he had caused her to have a fit. Right in the middle of his thrusting, she had dug her nails cruelly into his fat buttocks, sobbing through gritted teeth "O shit! . . . *shit* . . .! I'M COMING!"

Now as he sat so tantalising close to Gerda, his mind full of those exciting memories, his longing for her was almost unbearable. He felt himself breathing harder. God, how he would love to grab hold of her, push his hand up the skimpy skirt, plant his lips greedily on hers. But dare he? What would happen if they were discovered? Would she blab? One never knew with these little girls and even if the villagers didn't believe her there'd be talk, and that was something he had to avoid at all costs. When a man went 'underground' like he had done this summer, he didn't want attention drawn to himself in any way. He pressed his nails into the palms of his hands in frustration till it hurt.

Then Gerda said something which made all thoughts of ravishing her virginal body vanish immediately. She said, "While you were upstairs doing things to *Mutti*, there was a man looking through the panel in the door *Onkel* Alois."

He started, his erection vanishing at once. "What? What kind of man?" he demanded.

She looked at him, abruptly frightened by his gruff manner. *Onkel* Alois had never spoken to her like that before. She pouted and muttered, "Just a man."

"From here . . . from the village?"

She shook her head, tears in her eyes.

He pressed her hand with faked tenderness. "Now Gerda, I didn't mean to hurt you. You see the man could have been some kind of pervert. There are men who like to see other people, er, doing things."

"You mean Peeping Toms?"

"Yes, that's it. I have to protect you and naturally *Mutti* too. So what did this man look like?"

119

"I only saw his reflection in the mirror over there for a few seconds. But he was wearing dark glasses – like ski glasses – though there's no sun today, *Onkel*. I thought that was a bit funny."

Barsch felt a cold finger of fear trace its way down his spine. He hadn't taken the little local train to Garmisch as ordered. He had thought they might go away, but they hadn't. The man with the dark glasses and weeping eye-socket had come back. And with the certainty of an instant vision, Barsch knew that he had come back for him.

Gerda looked up at his suddenly pale face. "Everything all right, *Onkel* Alois?"

"Yes," he answered hurriedly and rose to his feet. "I just have to go over to the inn for a few moments." He reached for his jacket.

"*Onkel* Alois," she said, while above her mother snored loudly, "you will do nice things to me like you do to *Mutti* soon, won't you?"

"Yes, yes," he snapped swiftly, though doing 'nice things' to Gerda was furthest from his mind at this moment. Then he pulled on his hat and was gone, as if the Devil himself was after him.

Chapter Seven

Slowly the two jeeps ground up the winding mountain road that led to the ex-German Army's mountain infantry's barracks, the *Gebirgsjagerkaserne*. The scenery was spectacular. On both sides there were lush-green mountain valleys, and beyond the wooded slopes of firs, like rank after rank of spike-helmeted Prussian soldiers, leading to the jagged ridges and snow-capped peaks of the Wetterstein mountains.

The air was cold but like wine and as tired as they were from their long journey across Bavaria, they savoured it like they might a tonic, their weariness vanishing as they sucked it in.

"Impressive!" Rory, who was not an imaginative or very sensitive man, was forced to admit. "You couldn't think of something untoward happening in places like this."

Smith, who had even less of an imagination, commented, "All right for scenery, Boss. But you know Old Jerry, he can cause frigging trouble anywhere, even in heaven."

"Suppose you're right, Smithy," Rory said and, falling silent, continued to enjoy the scenery as they climbed even higher, noting as they did so that, although Mittenwald was close to the tourist area of Garmisch, there seemed to be few houses about.

The place was definitely remote. So far they had seen two farmhouses and on the road itself they had encountered a few foreign refugees and one solitary farmer in leather shorts herding his fat cows, their bells tinkling as they headed back for the night's milking. These days no farmer in his right mind would leave his animals out overnight on the lush meadows. They wouldn't be there in the morning if he did.

They swung round the bend and there was the *Gebirgsjagerkaserne*, looking rundown and shabby, though, as Rory told himself, a lot more modern than the 18th Century barracks in which he had spent most of his time in Britain. The jeeps started to slow down. A GI who had been lounging against the wall next to the gate, tossed away his cigarette and picked up his carbine. Yawning and obviously bored, his black face a little pinched in the late afternoon cold, he said in a slow Southern drawl, "You all got orders?"

Rory nodded and held up the papers which Joe Rosenblum had obtained for them from his lady friend and the sentry nodded. "Okay, pass friend," he said and then leaned back against the wall, tilted his helmet down above his eyes and promptly went back to sleep.

"Not exactly the Brigade of Guards, Smithy," Rory said as they drove into the barracks, where a group of black mechanics were hammering away listlessly at the track of a Sherman tank, watched by an NCO, who for some reason was wearing sun-glasses. No one took the slightest bit of notice of them.

"Well, they're harmless," the big ex-Guardsman answered, "and they won't ask any *awkward* questions to my way of thinking."

"That's my thought, too," Rory agreed as Smith 175 started to pull up in front of the orderly room (though

122

by now they had learned to call it, American style, 'the company office').

"Joe," Rory ordered, "you come with me. See if we can't get you permission to call your lady friend in Frankfurt."

"Yes Boss," Rosenblum answered eagerly.

They went in and pushed open a kind of little gate to where a giant black was slumped in a chair, his boots unbuckled, and his face buried in the US Army newspaper *The Stars and Stripes*.

"Who's in charge here?" Rory asked briskly in the fashion of the British Army.

Slowly, very slowly, the big black lowered the newspaper and stared at them, no emotion visible on his shining, moonlike face. Again very slowly he jerked his thumb at his own chest and said, "I is."

"*You?*" Rory took in the sloplly-looking man with his shirt unbuttoned and the stump of an unlit cigar, with the band still on, secured in the right-hand corner of his thick-lipped mouth.

"Yeah, cos I's the big nig! What do you want, limey?"

"Food and petrol. A place for the night and a telephone call to Shaef HQ in Frankfurt."

The 'Big Nig' nodded his agreement. "Have you got orders?" he said, asking the same question as the sleepy sentry at the gate.

Rory nodded. "Then you've got everything. Parachutists, eh?" the 'Big Nig' enquired looking at the blue and white jump wings of the SAS.

"Sort of."

The big Negro captain's round face lit up. "Good guys, paratroopers. Saved mah ass at Bastogne last December. Okay, go over to the mess hall and get some chow. I'll fix the cots for you and you can call Frankfurt from the signals shack."

The 'Big Nig' raised his *Stars and Stripes* and started reading the 'funnies' once more, his visitors obviously forgotten.

They were eating a strange mixture of fried eggs – "God," Smith 175 had exclaimed, "as many fried eggs as you can eat! This is paradise" – and buckwheat flapjack with maple syrup when Joe Rosenblum came back from the radio shack looking shocked and worried.

Rory put down his knife and fork immediately and beckoned him over to where he and Miles were eating at a separate table. "What's the matter, Joe?"

"It's Lisa, my lady friend, Boss," Joe stammered and Rory could see there were tears in his dark eyes.

"What's wrong with her, Joe?" Rory asked, looking at Miles in a puzzled fashion. "Here, come and sit down, Joe." He pushed a chair forward.

"Thank you," Joe sighed gratefully and collapsed into the chair. "She's dead – *murdered*!"

"What?" Miles and Rory exclaimed in unison.

"Yes. I talked to her boss. She was murdered yesterday afternoon in her office. Someone walked in and slit . . ." Joe's voice trembled badly, . . . "her throat."

"In broad daylight in Eisenhower's HQ?" Rory gasped.

"That's what worries her boss, sir. The place is heavily guarded. It's still like wartime. After all a lot of Jerries must hold a grudge against Eisenhower so they take very strict security precautions. So how could anyone get in and do that—" He broke off, unable to continue, his face buried in his hands, while the black cook with the frying pan at the end of the messhall continued mixing his batter and stared at them in bewilderment.

For a moment there was a heavy, brooding silence, while they thought the matter over. Their appetite had vanished now. The food started to grow cold on the tin plates. There was something eerie about this terrible murder.

Rory O'Sullivan, his forehead creased in a bewildered frown, finally broke the silence. "It's obvious who did it would have to have had some American identification to get inside the place, probably an American uniform, too." He sucked his front teeth thoughtfully for a second. "Now let's concentrate on the problem at hand for a moment. We already know that an American is mixed up in this strange business. So if we can find out here how that tank was allowed to leave the place, we might get a lead."

Miles shook his head. "It's all so very confusing and mysterious," he complained. "We set off to find that murdering swine Barsch and we end up unravelling some kind of organisation that has both US and Jerry links."

Rory said, "I know. But I think I must have a word with that fat captain first." He pushed away his half-eaten plate and the black cook looked offended.

"You don't like my chow, Cap'n?" he asked in an aggrieved tone. "I could rustle you up a fresh batch of flapjacks if you like."

Rory shook his head. "No thank you, cook. It was very fine food indeed. Best we've eaten in a long time."

"Yes," Tashy Kennedy agreed. "Never had so many fried eggs in all my life! Where we come from, mate, it's one egg a week per person, *per-haps*."

The cook's grin returned and he said, "Thank you gentlemen," following the words with a slight bow

125

as if he were the chef of a great hotel who had just been complimented on his cooking by some personality.

Rory waited till the cook had returned to the kitchen behind the swing doors, then he said, "We're not stopping here after all. The least contact we have with the Yanks in Bavaria the better. I'm sure you'll all agree after this shocking murder?"

They nodded, faces set and grim, while Joe Rosenblum stared into nothing.

"Miles," Rory turned to his nephew, "I want you to get the jeeps fuelled up and see if you can cadge some rations, especially cigarettes, from that cook. He seems a nice fellow."

"Will do."

"All right," Rory put on his maroon beret, "I'm going to see him now, but be ready for a swift departure, just in case." Then he was gone.

The fat captain was still reading the 'funnies' when Rory knocked and went into the company office once more, and those big feet were still propped on the desk. He looked up and asked, "Did my boys feed you okay?"

"Yes, Captain, very well indeed. Excellent!"

"Swell! What can I do for you? But take a seat first."

Hastily Rory drew up a chair, with the carved *Edelweiss*, the emblem of the German Alpine trrops, on the back.

"This." Rory decided to come straight to the point. The sun was already beginning to sink behind the mountains and the dark shadows of approaching night were racing across the alpine meadows. "We were attacked by a Sherman that originated from

126

this depot and which was driven by some Germans, all dead now," he added grimly.

The 'Big Nig' dropped his *Stars and Stripes* as if he had been genuinely surprised. "Say again?" he demanded.

Rory did so and the black captain scratched the back of his shaven head in obvious bewilderment. "Well," he drawled, "if that isn't the darndest thing!"

"Yes, but how could those Germans get the Sherman out of this place? It's not easy to steal a 30-ton tank, is it?"

The black captain bit his bottom lip. "Mister, you've gotta understand what's going on here around Garmisch. I've heard the guys call it 'Dodge City'. It's the Wild West all over again. The things that go on there turn your hair grey."

"The Sherman?" Rory attempted to stop him, but the black man wasn't listening.

"They say there's millions in gold bars, US dollars, your English pounds, buried in the woods all around here. Everybody seems to be on the take. The fixers, the go-betweens, they can buy anybody and anything they want. Even poor coloured folk can get in on the act these days, if the bad guys need something badly enough."

"You mean that someone bribed one of your chaps to let them have that Sherman?"

The black man looked worried. Tiny pearls of sweat had formed at the base of his hairline and he licked his lips, as if they had suddenly gone very dry. "I'm not saying that exactly, mister," he replied carefully. "But it could have been something like. Women, dollars, drugs – some of the boys smoke. And you can see just how slack the discipline is here. I can't control them. They're drunk most of the time as it is or going AWOL to shack

127

up with their whores. Anybody – *anything* – could go through them gates and they wouldn't notice or if they did they wouldn't care. What's a goddam Sherman to them? They didn't allow us fight 'em during the war. We were just shit-shovellers from Louisiana," he added bitterly, "no-good black trash. So why should the boys worry about their goddam useless tanks now?"

Rory could see the bitter resentment burning from the black captain's eyes and he said swiftly, "I take your point. But do you think that there was someone – or some group in particular – behind the theft of the Sherman?"

The black captain leaned forward urgently. "Yeah, I think I do."

"Go on."

"Well, down in Garmisch there is an old German guy—"

The phone on his desk jingled urgently. He picked it up and snapped, "Yeah?"

Suddenly he sat very straight, as if he were talking to someone very important. When he spoke his voice lacked that casual Southern drawl. In its place he was sharp and military. "Yes sir! I understand, sir. No sir, I haven't said anything. Wilco, sir." He put the phone down and Rory could see he was breathing hard, as if he had just run a race. There was fear in his bloodshot eyes, too.

"Problems?" Rory asked.

"Yeah, for you."

"What?"

"I'm not saying no more except get the hell outa here while you're still got time, buddy." Then 'Big Nig' rose swiftly, went into the inner office and bolted the door behind him.

128

Chapter Eight

"He's coming up the drive," Dieter said. He pressed the blind man's hand. "You will be careful. I don't trust him altogether."

Der Blinde chuckled. It wasn't a pleasant sound. "He has been bought. We can send him to one of his own prisons if we reveal what he is doing to those damned decadent Americans. Besides, we have our other precautions, haven't we, Dieter my darling!" He reached out, felt for the boy's soft hand with its lacquered nails and pressed it affectionately.

Dieter said, "Yes, I suppose. But I don't like the thought of having him killed in here." He indicated the great room with its ancient masters on the walls and the Gobelins, although he knew his lover couldn't see the drawing-room.

"Rest assured, it won't ever come to that. Besides, this cowboy general of theirs, Patton, trusts him implicitly – and any German who he feels is prepared to fight the Reds, whether they were members of the Party or not." *Der Blinde*'s keen ears heard the squeak of the brake as the jeep pulled up. "Prepare him something to drink, Dieter," he ordered.

For a few moments, the tall German-American Colonel and the blind man chatted idly while the former sipped his drink. He really wasn't a drinking

129

man, but toying with the glass gave him time to marshall his thoughts, for he knew that in *Der Blinde* he was dealing with the most cunning and powerful man in Garmisch, perhaps in the whole of this part of Bavaria.

He knew little about the German, who could be any age, for he had a strangely unlined, almost boyish, face, but he had to be old for he had been one of the founder members of the National Socialist Party, one of a handful who had been allowed to address Hitler in private with the familiar 'thou'. How the German had been blinded he did not know. Some said in the bombing of Munich; others that he had been blinded long before that when a communist had thrown acid in his face before 1933 when Hitler had taken over power in Germany. What Ziller did know was that *Der Blinde* would stop at nothing: blackmail, bribery, murder, to achieve his aim, which was to arrange for a continuation of the beaten Third Reich.

Ziller put down his glass. It was time to discuss business, he told himself, and find out why he had been summoned here so hastily. Normally the two of them met under conditions of great secrecy. Today the German had asked him to drive up to his villa immediately and without any special arrangements being made.

Der Blinde heard the sound of the glass being placed on the table between them and must have sensed by Ziller's breathing, too, that the Colonel was ready to talk. He beat Ziller to it. Quite categorically, as if it was a simple statement of fact, he said, "Your Army in Germany, Colonel Ziller, is in complete disarray. The Army of Occupation is out of control of its officers. Both officers and enlisted men live off the black market. The men are drunk most of the time. Ordinary German civilians are, quite frankly, scared of them, they are always brawling and fighting in the streets. Last week 3,000 GIs demonstrated in front of Eisenhower's office in Frankfurt crying 'We wanne go home . . . we wanne go home!'" He imitiated the cry in English contemptuously.

Ziller looked solemn and uncomfortable.

"Dieter here tells me that the *New York Times* has written of them recently, that the occupation army is 'an aggregation of homesick Americans shirking their jobs to figure out ways of making money . . . German troops occupying France during the war had a better record in their personal contact with the population than the American troops occupying Germany'." He paused to let his words sink in.

Ziller said, "Yes, I know. The situation is dreadful."

Der Blinde didn't even seem to notice that he had spoken. He continued: "At the moment that is a problem for your people. But once the communist threat to Germany becomes more acute, which it will, then the state of the soldiers becomes my concern. Time is running out. We must be prepared for what will surely come when you Americans will definitely need us Germans."

"I agree most strongly with you," Ziller said enthusiastically.

"Dieter," *Der Blinde* tapped the table, "another drink for the Colonel."

Dieter appeared as if by magic, as if he had been waiting there all the time, bearing another full glass on the shining silver tray. He put it down, saying, "*Prost Herr Oberst.*" As he passed the blind man he pressed his shoulder affectionately.

131

Ziller pulled a face, but said nothing. Still he didn't like that sort of thing.

"So," *Der Blinde* continued, when he guessed that Ziller had taken the first sip of his new drink, "you know by now that we have millions of dollars in gold bullion hidden in the mountains and forests all around Garmisch."

Ziller did, though he didn't know where even after extensive clandestine operations instigated by no less than General Patton. Two months before he had been summoned to Patton's HQ at Bad Toelz. Patton had been in a bad temper. He had strode back and forth in his big office, followed by his ugly dog Willie, all the time slapping one highly polished riding boot with his crop. "Ziller," he had snorted, "some news for you. This Major Allgeier here," he pointed to what was obviously a German Jew dressed in US uniform and wearing the flaming sword insignia of Shaef, "has made me cognisant that most of the treasure of the German State Bank is hidden somewhere in my Third Army area."

The Jew had nodded but had said nothing.

Patton had continued with, "I want that hoard found. The whole fuckin' lot has to be discovered and sent back to Ike in Frankfurt." He had chuckled, showing his dingy, sawn-off teeth. "And when you do, send the padre with the shipment to pray all the ways that it gets there safely."

A week later, *Der Blinde* had allowed him to 'find' a crate of US dollar bills, which he had conveyed to Patton who had called him and rasped, "Peanuts, just peanuts! A million bucks won't buy 30 seconds of total war on the black market. *Find the rest, Ziller!*"

Now it was clear that the strange, youthful-looking

blind man was going to reveal more about the fabled hoard.

"The situation is becoming acute," *Der Blinde* went on. "Those Jews in Frankfurt are getting too close for my liking." He grinned, showing his gold teeth. "With your help I had to have one of them murdered. A woman. We had her throat slit to warn the others off. She was a Jewess naturally."

Zeller bit his bottom lip, suddenly very worried. So that's why they had wanted the pass into Shaef HQ, with which he had provided them. Things were getting hot.

"Now the Tommies have turned up, as you know. I think they're on to something too."

"Yes, I know," Ziller agreed and took a hefty gulp at his drink. "I had to warn the commander of the depot from which the Sherman came not to give them any more information."

Der Blinde was not impressed. "The Tommies are a shrewd people. One should never underestimate them. I think that warning might well have fuelled their suspicions even more. But no more." He held up his soft, feminine hand as if to stop any protest on Ziller's part.

Ziller fell silent immediately.

"Now, as I have said, we shall have to move and move soon. I am sure that Frankfurt will send more of those German Jewish spies into this area to find out what's going on, as soon as they can find suitable cover. Colonel Ziller," he raised his voice, "if you were going to send a large shipment into Switzerland," he didn't say what the shipment would be, but Ziller guessed he meant gold bullion and foreign currency, "what route would you select? And bear this in mind, there are

American troops occupying the German border with the former *Ostmark** too."

Ziller didn't consider for more than a second. He knew already that the 'Spider Organisation', which he guessed the blind man controlled, was sending wanted Nazis over the border into Austria. From there they moved ports to the south of Italy, from where they were shipped to South America. *Reichs-fuhrer* Martin Bormann himself was supposed to have used this route, the 'B-B Route', – Bolzano–Bari as it was called. "It is still the Austrian-Italian route. The GIs can't control all the mountain passes and there are plenty of bribable border guards in both Austria and Italy, as you know well."

"Exactly. But this would not be individuals, but a regular convoy," *Der Blinde* objected.

Ziller pursed his lips. In the outer room a gramophone was playing a record of one of those sentimental *schmalzig* love songs popular in the war, and by the sound of it the perverted youngster Dieter was dancing to the music.

Der Blinde heard it too and allowed himself a smile. "The boy must have his little pleasures," he commented gently. "It can't be much fun for him looking after a grumpy old cripple like me. But back to our problem."

A little confused, Colonel Ziller said, "I'm really at a loss. How do you get a convoy of gold out of the Third Army area by any different route than the shortest?"

Der Blinde chuckled. "You think that the transport would be stopped by your white mice?", meaning the white-helmeted US military police.

* The Nazi name for Austria.

134

"Exactly."

"They wouldn't if they were American trucks and they had the proper orders." *Der Blinde* chuckled again knowingly. "Especially if the white mice were given nice little presents – in the form of dollar bills – not to be over particular."

Ziller whistled softly. "You mean—"

"Yes, I do! You would provide the trucks."

Ziller wanted to object, but thought better of it for the moment. He'd meet that particular obstacle when it became more acute. "So what route do you suggest?"

"Black Forest, French Zone of Occupation." He made the Continental gesture of counting money with his thumb and forefinger. "The French, too, are as corrupt as you *Amis*. They can be bought, and then through Alsace and over the border into Switzerland. What ordinary French gendarme is going to stop a convoy of American trucks? Why should they, especially if they are taking country routes where there are only villages and odd hamlets."

"I see." Ziller pondered the suggestion for a few moments. Outside in the other room the music had stopped, but Ziller could smell the strong odour of female perfume wafting under the door. The perverted kid was obviously dousing himself with it for some reason and he could guess it was for something that would happen after he left. What goddam perverts they were, the two of them!

"I have knowledge of a man," *Der Blinde* went on, "who knows the backroads of Alsace like the back of his hand. Not too well expressed, but he does. He is not a brave man, not one of us. A time-server and a deserter. But for the time being we need him for his

135

knowledge. This man, Barsch, is being brought here. He will work out the route to be taken, while you start organising the vehicles and the necessary papers."

"It's going to be a tall order!"

Der Blinde wasn't impressed. "It has to be done," he said simply, with an air of finality. Suddenly there was iron in his voice. "*And it will be done!*" he added harshly.

"Yes, yes, of course," Ziller agreed hastily.

"You will meet this man when he has worked out the route. You will need to know the details so you can deal with logistics of the journey."

"Yes – his name?

"Barsch, *Herr Doktor* Barsch," the German emphasised the title contemptuously. "One of *those* fools, but at the moment he is a useful fool. Thank you for coming." Ziller was dismissed.

Just as he was about to get into his jeep, Ziller looked back at the villa. Silhouetted against the wall of the great salon, magnified by the flickering shadows coming from the great open fire, he saw their shadows. They were dancing together . . .

Chapter Nine

The streets were thinning out of civilians in Garmisch as curfew time neared and those who could gain nothing from staying out after nine, meaning those who had no dealings with the *Amis*, were on their way home. A cold wind was blowing in from the mountains and there would be a frost tonight. All the same, as Joe Rosenblum walked the streets slowly, followed by the gigantic bulk of Sergeant Smith 175 as his bodyguard, the two of them could hear plenty of noise coming from the many inns: loud American raucous laughter, the drunken screams and giggles of women, "*Ami whores*," Joe had heard the locals call them scornfully. 'Dodge City' in Bavaria was living up to its reputation this cold night.

Smith fell in beside the little SAS trooper. "Remember what the Boss, said, Joe," he warned. "This is supposed to be only a recce. We want no trouble. We—"

He didn't finish his warning. A drunken GI staggered out of the door of an inn opposite, followed by a blast of loud music. He pushed by Smith and Rosenblum blindly, threatening, "Get outa ma way, you fucking Krauts, or I'll punch yer heads in" to disappear into the night.

"Polite sort of geezer," Smith 175 said without

rancour, knowing that he could have knocked the drunken GI's teeth out with one hand tied behind his back.

"Come on," Joe urged, not wanting to attract any attention to himself, for he was quite convinced now that this Colonel Ziller poor Lisa had mentioned was hand in glove with the Germans, and Ziller would undoubtedly control whatever law and order still existed in 'Dodge City'.

They headed for the big inn, filled with drunken laughter and the sound of Harry James belting out *The Boogie-Woogie Bugleboy of Company B*. Inside, they were met by a blue fug of cigarette smoke and the sight of German girls being thrown all over the floor by sweating drunken GIs as they gyrated and twisted hectically to the 'music'.

"Christ all-frigging mighty!" Smith 175 exclaimed in awed wonder, as a big hulking GI threw a screaming girl over his shoulder to reveal that she was wearing no knickers. And she wasn't the only one. "There's more naked beaver in here, Joe, than in a cheap Cairo knocking shop," he said.

A flustered waiter bearing huge steins of local beer pushed by them saying in broken English in a worried manner, "Pliz, sit at back of ze room. This a GI bar. No place for others. We don't want no trouble, no pliz."

Joe shrugged and together with Smith they pushed their way through the loud, drunken, sweating mob to a small table at the wall, where no one sat, obviously because the view of the dance floor was obscured by the wooden pillar in front of it.

They sat down at the plain wooden table awash with beer suds and waited. Waiters and waitresses in Bavarian costume, their huge breasts half hanging out of their tight dirndl bodices, rushed back and forth carrying ever more beer for the thirsty GIs, though the two SAS troopers noticed that most of them also had quarts of bourbon and scotch on their tables as well. But the waiters seemed to pay no attention to the two soldiers in the shadows, wearing the unfamiliar uniform.

Smith 175 licked his lips enviously and said, "Joe, I could just go a pint of that wallop."

In the end Joe Rosenblum lost his patience. He glared at one of the waiters, tossed ten cigarettes on the table and rasped harshly, "*Zwei Mass, Herr Ober und ein bisschen schnell . . . Los!*"

The waiter looked for an instant as if he might refuse, then he saw the look on Joe's face and changed his mind. Minutes later they had two great foaming mugs of Bavarian beer in front of them and the waiter wiped the table clean, too.

So they sat there, observing the crowd, realising that if these GIs were typical of the whole of the Third Army then Bavaria was in a mess. Anything seemed to go. There were drunks everywhere, sprawled with their crew-cut heads in pools of stale beer. GIs sat with women on their knees, hands up their skirts openly fondling them. On all sides GIs were brazenly carrying out black market deals, selling cigarettes and cans of coffee for jewellery, gold coins and other precious items. In a corner two cursing, red-faced GIs were writhing on the floor punching each other relentlessly, blood streaming from their noses. Nobody seemed to take a bit of notice.

Smith wiped the suds from his mouth and said, "Joe, this little lot is a regular shower of shit. I don't think we're gonna find out much here for the Boss 'cept that

139

the US Army in Bavaria seems to have gone down the frigging tubes. Once we've finished this wallop we'd better move on, don'tcha think?"

Joe Rosenblum didn't answer immediately. Instead he kept his gaze on a small man, perhaps the only sober GI there, who sat close to the hectic, sweating jitterbuggers on the tiny dance floor, accompanied by two ravishing blondes who couldn't seem to keep their hands off his skinny body. They were all over him, kissing him on the side of the face, his lips, hands straying constantly to his lap, as if they couldn't get his trousers off quickly enough. And, unlike the rest of the GIs in the old inn, this one paid for his drinks and services with $5 bills, not in kind or the worthless Occupation marks. No wonder the flustered, overworked waiters and waitresses kept smiling and calling, "*Noch etwas, mein Herr?*"

Finally, Joe nudged Smith 175 as the little GI took out a huge roll of dollar bills and ordered yet more champagne for the two tipsy blondes – obviously beer was too common for his taste – and asked, "Anything strange about the Yank with the two Judies?"

Smith stared over the rim of his beer mug. "Not much I'd say, Joe, 'cept he seems to be doing very well with them two tarts. By the size of him you wouldn't think he'd be capable of handling both of them."

"I didn't mean that!" Joe snorted, a little irritated. "I mean the way he's flashing money about, the fact he's wearing the badges of the US Ordnance Corps – *and his looks!*" Rosenblum emphasised the last few words, as if they were of some significance.

Smith 175 frowned. "Well, he does look a bit like a darkie," he admitted, taking in the little man's yellow-brown skin and his shiny, pomaded black curly hair.

"You're telling me," Joe Rosenblum said firmly. "He *is* a darkie."

Smith shrugged his huge shoulders carelessly. "So what? There's a lot o' folk who's darkies in this world, Joe."

"You don't get the point," Joe argued.

Smith 175 chuckled and drained the rest of his beer happily, though just previously he'd remarked that it was "as weak as gnat's piss". "I bet them Judies are gonna get *his* point before the night's out, the way they keep touching up his goolies." He sighed. "Lovely grub!"

"It's not that," Joe said, his irritation growing by the instant, for he didn't tolerate fools gladly. "What's a darkie doing in a white Yanks' hangout in an Army where they hate darkies?"

Smith 175 looked serious and thoughtful. "I take your point."

"And why's he flashing all them readies and showing off with the white women?" Rosenblum answered his own question. "Cos that darkie's got clout. And he's in ordnance too. So where does he get the readies?"

"*The Sherman.*"

"Exactly! I just feel it, Sarge."

"Yer, just like that tart is feeling his at this very moment," Smith 175 interrupted with a wry grin, "and I wouldn't mind another pint of wallop if you could see your way to it, Trooper Rosenblum."

Rosenblum shared his grin, although his brain was racing. "Your wish is my command! You know what they say, old sarge. 'Crap sez the king and a thousand arseholes bent and took the strain for in them days the word of the king was law'."

Smith 175 shook his head in mock wonder. "For a

foreign Jewboy you speaks da lingo even better than what I does, matey."

After the beer was brought, Rosenblum continued, "That darkie's in here because he's got high-priced protection. Look at all them Yanks. They knock each other's block off just for a dirty look. So why don't they turf him out on his arse? I'll tell you why. Cos someone's looking after him, and it ain't a bloke in a white robe sitting on a frigging cloud playing his frigging harp!"

"Stands to reason, Joe," Smith 175 agreed, as he watched the GI sit back and allow one of the blondes to undo his flies and slide her hand in.

"So we nobble him," Joe Rosenblum decided.

Smith nodded his agreement. "As soon as those tarts are finished with him, which'll be soon by the look on his face, the lucky bugger! Look at that, the other tart's got it in her hand now!" he sighed enviously. "Some people have all the frigging luck. Ah well." He took another great swallow of beer, belched and added, "Ay, there's one law fer poor and another fer rich," as if that statement explained everything.

Ten minutes later the trim little black soldier left the inn, dropping $5 bills casually on the table for the waiter while the two blondes lifted their skirts and stuffed the $100 he had given each of them in the tops of their nylons. He stepped fastiously over the drunks snoring in pools of beer on the floor, circled the two angry, blood-stained GIs still pounding each other with their fists, and went outside to shiver in the sudden cold coming from the snow-capped mountains.

The two SAS men followed him cautiously. The little man put his fingers into his mouth and whistled shrilly three times. As if by magic, a Peep – a roofed jeep – came round the corner and braked to a halt.

"Christ Almighty!" Smith 175 gasped, as the door opened and a huge black man got out. "The cocky bugger's even got his own chauffeur!"

Joe nodded. "It looks like, Sarge," he agreed as the black giant opened the nearside door of the Peep for the little man to get in. "Anyway, let's nobble him. There's nobody about."

"Right. I'm all for that," Smith snorted. "That little bugger of a darkie's getting right up my nose. Come on, Joe!"

"That driver looks a big sod," Joe said a little hesitantly as they moved almost noiselessly through the shadows.

"The bigger the sods are the harder they fall Joe," Smith said scornfully. "You leave it to me. Just you attend to the cocky little shit. I'll sort the other darkie out."

Joe came out of the shadows and whined like a German on the make, "*Haben Sie eine Zigarette fur mich, Herr Soldat?*"

The little man turned. In the same instant, Smith 175, moving with surprising speed for such a big man, thrust his brawny right arm around the driver's neck and stuck his knee into the small of his back. The black giant was taken completely by surprise and Smith 175 didn't give him the chance to recover. He jerked hard, exerting all his strength, cutting off the man's supply of blood to his head. Suddenly he let go. The big black man staggered and gasped for air frantically. But Smith went into action. Grunting, "Sweet dreams, old mate," he clapped both big hands across the black man's ears sharply. It was an old SAS trick. Too hard and the

143

opponent would be dead on the spot, too softly and it wouldn't work. Smith 175 hit the happy medium. The black giant staggered once more, then fell to his knees like a boxer refusing to go down for the count. To no avail, next moment he slammed to the pavement face first, out like a felled ox.

Smith turned, a big grin over his broad face. Joe was standing in front of the terrified little man, his steel Army comb held just under his flared nostrils. "One word out of you, monkey face," he was whispering, "and I'll rip yer frigging face apart! Understand?"

Carefully, very carefully, which was to be expected with those deadly sharp steel teeth of the comb just beneath his nose, the little man nodded saying through gritted teeth, "Yes . . . understand."

Smith grinned, hardly panting now. "I'm proud of yer, Joe. Yer've learned a lot since yer've bin with our mob." He stepped over the unconscious body of the black giant and said to the petrified little man, "All right, sunshine, you're coming with us and we don't want you making no fuss. Or else—" He clenched a fist like a small steam shovel under the man's chin. "Right, here we go."

Thirty seconds later they had disappeared into the shadows, heading for the concealed SAS jeep. They now had their lead.

PART THREE

End Game

Chapter One

Barsch was very uneasy. As he sat there in the little office they had given him in the villa to work out a route into Switzerland, he caught glimpses of the strange visitors to the villa and the owners themselves.

There were black Americans who kept coming and going in jeeps and he was sure that half of them were drunk or doped or perhaps both. There was a white Colonel, named Ziller, who spoke German perfectly but in the clipped northern tones of a Prussian. Then there were Germans, armed, who prowled the grounds, carrying their machine-pistols openly though everyone knew that it was now an offence punishable with death for a German to carry a weapon.

But most disquieting of all was the owner of the villa, 'the blind one', as he called himself for he seemed to have no name, and his simpering powdered friend Dieter, with his painted nails and lips, who often held the older man's hand fondly. Barsch knew what they were, but unlike the other 'warm brothers' whom he had known in the past, these two exuded a sense of death. They might well posture and prance in the absurd, affected manner of homosexuals, but all the time he felt uneasy in their presence. There was the feeling about them that they could be absolutely ruthless if they wished, especially *Der Blinde*. Despite his soft unlined face he had the look of a man who was accustomed to giving orders, and having them obeyed immediately. Or else.

It was obvious, too, that he was in charge of the whole operation whatever it was. The armed guards, the blacks, were clearly scared of him. Even the hard-faced American colonel with his strict Prussian manner, who obviously disliked the perverted relationship between the older man and his boy friend, Dieter, was very deferential and sometimes even scared, that was clear.

Barsch bit his weak, sensual lower lip and felt he couldn't really concentrate on the map he was using to work out a route for some sort of convoy. He had taken a dive and thought he had been safe as the respected '*Herr Lehrer*' in that remote Bavarian village. Now he knew instinctively that he was in danger again.

"You will be well rewarded, *Herr Doktor*," the blind man had said after the man with the dark glasses and the weeping eye had introduced him and then promptly vanished, "if you do your job properly. But do not make any mistakes. That would annoy me." His voice had remained quite steady and without menace, but he had seen from the look in Dieter's eyes, under the plucked eyelashes and mascara, that it would be very, very dangerous, to cross his lover.

Four years of working as a Gestapo agent in France, using turncoats and renegades who been dispensed with when no longer useful, had taught him to sense the authorities' real intentions. Somehow he felt, it was a kind of sixth sense, that anyone connected with this mission, who would no longer be of any use after it was over, would be quietly dispensed with. What was the old saying? '*Dead men tell no tales.*' He felt he was going to be one of those dead men.

Outside, the big American Colonel was talking earnestly to the blind one, ignoring the blacks who lounged about laughing and giggling, as if they didn't have a care in the world, which at that moment they did not. Again Barsch, the expert in liquidation, knew they, too, were expendable. Once this mission was over they would suffer the same fate he anticipated for himself. The thought made him shiver with fear.

"Louse run over your liver, *Herr Doktor?*" a silky but sinister voice inquired behind him.

He turned, startled. It was Dieter, the blind one's lover. He had entered noiselessly on those rubber-soled shoes of his, 'Brothel-creepers', the soldiers of the *Wehrmacht* had called them.

"Just the shivers," he admitted.

"We must stoke the fires higher," Dieter said and though he smiled, his green eyes were wary, searching Barsch's plump weak face for something he, alone, knew was there. "You liked to stoke the fires at Natzweiler, they say," he added in a casual manner, referring to the only concentration camp on French soil at Natzweiler in Alsace.

Barsch blanched. "I had nothing to do with that," Barsch stammered, caught completely off guard. "I was a police officer, pure and simple, fighting the *Resistance* and—"

"Don't piss me," Dieter said, his voice suddenly hard. "We know all about you, Barsch." This time he didn't afford the other man his academic title, not that Barsch noticed. He was too frightened by this sudden attack.

"But," he stuttered, "Herr Dieter—"

149

"Knock it off," the young man with the plucked eyebrows said harshly. "Just listen to me. Don't try to shit us, because we can't be shat upon. We're too smart to be taken in by academic pisspots like you. Now answer me this question. Where do you think is the best spot for us to cross into Alsace?"

"Brisach . . . Neuf Brisach. That means New—" he started to explain.

Dieter cut him short with a brutal "I frigging well know what '*Neuf*' means, arse-with-ears! *Gut*, I'll tell that to the chief. He'll look into it this very afternoon. If you've done well he'll send you up a woman for tonight. Some Garmisch whore, no accounting for tastes. 'Fraid we can't deliver a schoolgirl to you. Too risky."

"But . . . but—"

Again Dieter cut him off with, "For chrissake, hold yer piss! We know *all* about you. And one more thing."

"What's that?"

"Don't think of trying to do a runner, *Herr Doktor*. Because if you do, you're a stiff – *a swift stiff!*"

"I never even thought of such thing—" Barsch started to bluster, but Dieter didn't even give him a chance to explain himself.

He cut in brutally with, "So you know where you stand, don't you now? It's *marschieren* or *krepieren* – march or croak." With that he was gone, leaving Barsch trembling.

Two hundred yards away, concealed in their hide, Miles and Rory surveyed the villa from above through their glasses. The little negro – 'high yallar', he called himself with some sort of obscure pride – had been very

150

informative, especially after Smith 175 had threatened to "get the Vaseline out and give him a bloody rogering up his black – high yallar, excuse me, gents – arse."

He had told them immediately what he had known, which hadn't been much, but enough. 'The Kraut faggots,' as he had called the blind man and his young campanion, were running some kind of illegal organisation. They had enough 'spondulicks' to bribe anyone they wanted to help them, including the big Colonel Ziller. "Boy, those guys buy anybody and everything," he had proclaimed in the accents of the Bronx. "Ya'd think they was Macey's!"

"But what are they up to?" Rory O'Sullivan had persisted. "That's what we want to know."

The little black had learned by now that these tough-looking limeys weren't really going to harm him and he was at ease. So he had scratched his head in a bewildered sort of way before saying, "As I said before, Cap'n, I don't know too much, 'cept about the Sherman tank thing." Hastily he had added, "Honest Injun, I didn't know they was gonna use it to take you guys out."

"Get on with it," Rory had urged. "I'll take your word for it."

"But all I know is that it's something to do with gold, lots of it."

"Gold, how do you mean?" Rory had persisted.

"Gold and US trucks," the little man had answered a little helplessly. "That's about all I can tell ya, Cap'n."

And with that they had been forced to be content.

Now, as they viewed the activity below, they realised that although they hadn't been able to get very much information out of their captive, he had been right.

151

Something big was going on. The question was, *WHAT?*

But as mystified as they were, the two secret watchers concerned themselves with registering mentally the faces of those who seemed in command down below at the villa. The blind man was obviously blind, though he didn't wear the usual yellow-and-black-dotted armband of the blind which they had seen often enough since the war in Germany. Then there was the harshly handsome American colonel, whom they now knew was Ziller who poor dead Lisa Hausmann, Joe's murdered 'lady friend', had mentioned. There was a cross-eyed fellow, armed with – of all things – a British Sten gun and carrying it openly, who seemed to be in charge of the armed men guarding the place. And then there was the mincing handsome 'Nancy Boy', as they had already nicknamed him, who was obviously the lover of the blind man in charge. He came and went constantly but each time he came out to where the blind boss was issuing his orders, he couldn't seem to keep his delicate white hands off the older man. "God Almighty, Rory!" Miles hissed once. "You'd think by the way he fondles the other bugger that he was Clark Gable himself!"

Rory gave a little shrug as they crouched there in the cover of the fir trees that marched up the slope of the mountains in rigid ranks, and whispered, "Money and power, Miles, old chap. They're supposed to be the world's most effective aphrodisiacs."

"Yes, suppose you're right. Hey, who's this the Nancy Boy's bringing out now? At three o'clock, Rory."

Hurriedly Rory O'Sullivan swung his glasses round in the direction indicated by his nephew. A fat, weak face came into the circle of calibrated glass. His heart missed a beat. He gasped.

Miles looked at him curiously. "What is it, Rory?" he asked swiftly.

For a long moment his uncle didn't answer, as he remembered the moment when he had last seen that pudgy face before his world had seemed to fall apart at the bridge over the River Rhine at Kehl.

"*Rory?*"

"I'm not quite one hundred per cent sure," he said, as if talking to himself.

"About what, Rory?" Miles asked urgently, taking in the pudgy, bespectacled German who was talking earnestly to the blind man while the 'Nancy Boy' looked on.

"Him."

"For God's sake, Rory, what's so special about the Hun?"

Rory swallowed hard and lowered his glasses. "It's him," he said finally. "*That man is Herr Doktor Barsch, the man we've come to get . . .*"

Chapter Two

The former Imperial Chief-of-Staff watched Churchill as he wallowed in his bath, smoking a cigar, with his false teeth in a glass next to the tub. Outside, the birds at Churchill's country house were busy singing their dawn chorus and the dour Ulsterman, Field Marshal Alanbrooke, who had had many an argument with Churchill about strategy during the war, wished fervently that he could be out in the garden watching the birds, his hobby, rather than waste his time in the smoke-heavy bathroom. But he felt a sense of loyalty for the great man who had seen Britain through to victory and then had been cruelly deposed.

Churchill dipped the end of his cigar in the glass of brandy set handily to his right and took a hearty puff, looking like some pink-skinned, toothless Buddha as he did so. "Well, what news of my Secret Hunters?" he asked.

Alanbrooke, who still kept his contacts with old friends in the War Office, though he, too, had been replaced on such a poor pension that he was considering having to sell his beloved books on birds to make ends meet, answered: "They are making progress according to the signal which reached the War House yesterday, PM."

Churchill waved his cigar at him. "Not PM any longer. Just plain Churchill, Field Marshal."

The Ulsterman's dour features coloured a little. "Of course, I forgot."

"I never will," Churchill remarked, his face suddenly sombre. "But no matter! Pray continue."

"They have found the man they went out to find, that is, they know his location. They've discovered something else, too. There seems to be some connivance between certain American officers and Germans to carry out a combined mission which is seemingly very important to the Germans concerned."

Churchill took another thoughtful puff at his big cigar. He exhaled a blue smoke ring and asked, "What is this mission exactly, my dear Alanbrooke?" His mood was suddenly enlivened and the Ulsterman, who had known him so long, could see that his mind, alert as it was for such an old man, was going off on one of its tangents, which he had cursed so often in the past.

"They don't know yet. But O'Sullivan, who as you know is in charge of the party, is certain that it is something big to judge from the resources they are putting into it. Considerable sums of foreign currency are apparently changing hands, according to the radio signal."

Churchill considered for a few moments before saying, "You know, my dear Field Marshal, I have a special place in my heart for the Special Air Service."

Alanbrooke said nothing. He disapproved of such irregular formations like the commandos and the SAS, they drained the best men away from regular battalions. He had always opposed Churchill on the issue, but during the war Churchill had been all-powerful. He had approved the commandos, the Parachute Regiment and the SAS. In Alanbrooke's opinion it was a good thing that they were now being stood down, save for the Parachute Regiment.

Churchill caught his look and smiled. "Yes, yes, I know what you think, Alanbrooke. But you know that a few determined bold young men can sometimes do more than a whole infantry battalion. In the desert in '42 the SAS destroyed more enemy planes on the ground than the whole of the RAF did in the air. You didn't know that, did you? But no matter."

Alanbrooke shook his greying head, but said nothing.

"So, dear Field Marshal," Churchill continued, obviously quite pleased with himself, "I think something ought to be done about these SAS chaps in Germany."

"How do you mean, sir?"

By way of answer Churchill said, "Please hand me that towel. The tub's getting cold."

To anyone else Alanbrooke would have been outraged, "I'm a British Field Marshal, not a bloody flunkey!" But not to Churchill. Tamely he handed over the big, fleecy white bathtowel.

Completely without shame, exhibiting his totally hairless white body, the ex-premier stepped from the bath and began towelling himself. Damnit, the Ulsterman cursed to himself, he'll be wanting his bloody vest handed to him next. That was exactly what Churchill asked for as soon as he was dry. "Be a good chap," he said, smiling his toothless smile, "and give me my vest. It's getting a little chilly in here."

Wordlessly the Field Marshal handed it over and Churchill put it on, with the silk vest not quite covering his plump buttocks. Not that that worried him, for he was completely without modesty in such matters. As he always maintained "morality is something for the lower middle class, they tell me."

"You see, Alanbrooke," he continued as he began towelling his legs, "if these SAS chaps can pull off a scoop, the War Office powers-that-be might well be convinced to re-instate the regiment."

Alanbrooke pulled a face. "Why, sir?" he queried. "Why do we need such regiments as the SAS?"

"I shall tell you," Churchill said, stepping into his silk underwear. "Because units like the SAS are the fighting units of the future, whatever the brasshats at the War House think – they've always been one war behind. We've got something called the Welfare State coming up. If we're not careful we'll sacrifice our empire in order to pay for granny's glasses and grandpa's false teeth. We simply won't be able to afford large-scale military formations. So we'll have to fight to preserve all that red on the map with small-scale elite formations like the SAS."

Alanbrooke considered for a moment and conceded a little reluctantly, "I suppose in a way you're right, sir."

"Of course I'm right, Alanbrooke! The socialists are going to ruin this country in the end, mark my words. If we let them we'll be a little island off the shores of Europe."

For the first time since Churchill's defeat at the polls in the general election, the dour Field Marshal could feel the ex-PM's resentment at the way he had been treated by the electorate.

Churchill completed his dressing in silence while Alanbrooke listened to the twittering of the birds outside, glad he was finished with grand strategy

157

and the interference of politics, wondering all the same what Churchill was up to now.

Churchill adjusted his tie and then told him. "Field Marshal," he said deliberately, "I'd like to use you as a sounding board."

"Sir?"

"Obviously the Americans, the corrupt ones, are involved in this business, too. So the American authorities should really take some interest in it and aid our chaps who are out there doing the spade work. Now am I to show my hand and contact Patton to tell him what's going on and ask him to offer assistance to our SAS people?" He looked enquiringly at the Ulsterman.

Alanbrooke considered for a few moments before saying, "Well, sir, if you do and it comes out, there are those now in power at the War Office who will find to their amazement that the SAS hasn't been disbanded in reality. That *will* set the cat among the pigeons."

Churchill grinned at him mischievously, like a cheeky schoolboy who had been found with his fingers in the jampot. "I am sure it will," he agreed. "But at the same time if O'Sullivan's people make a success of it and pull off some grand coup or other, it might influence future decisions about the fate of the Special Air Service."

Alanbrooke gave a little sigh. The former prime minister was playing politics again. He was hardly out of office and had now been demoted to being the leader of His Majesty's Opposition, yet he was already trying to influence policy, albeit through the back door.

"You disapprove?"

"No sir. Besides I'm in no position to approve or disapprove. But remember this, sir. Patton is rabidly

158

anti-British. Although he is independently wealthy, a former cavalry officer who once ran a string of polo ponies in the '30's, so that he's more like one of our upper-crust Household Cavalry toffs than any other American senior officer I met during the last show. But he still can't stand us and what he thinks is our antiquated class system. One will have to treat Patton with kid gloves if we hope to get him to co-operate with our chaps."

"Might not a little blackmail help?" Churchill asked softly, a deceptively benign look in his faded eyes.

"*Blackmail*, sir?" Alanbrooke looked aghast at the former premier.

"Well, in the past few years Intelligence has collected quite a few juicy titbits on the conduct of the American senior generals in Europe. There is this business of Eisenhower with his – er – secretary-cum-driver Kay Summersby. I am sure that wouldn't go down too well with the people back home in the United States. We know all about 'Beetle' Smith" – meaning Eisenhower's Chief-of-Staff – "and his nurses." He cleared his throat. "Then there was Patton's lady from the landed gentry last year when his HQ was in Cheshire. Now I am reliably informed that his current mistress is his niece, an American Red Cross worker."

Alanbrooke, who was very straight-laced, looked at Churchill aghast. "But, sir, you couldn't use that kind of dirty trick could you!"

Churchill nodded smugly. "If necessary," he said quietly. "You know with these senior American generals, we are dealing with middle-aged one-time obscure men who back in 1941 were contemplating a slippered retirement somewhere cheap. Suddenly they became public figures, known to everyone in the western world. Now they are running scared, Field Marshal. They can't afford any scandal or it'll be back to that slippered obscurity of four years ago. You understand?" Churchill smiled winningly at him.

Alanbrooke frowned and tugged at the end of his nose as his thoughts raced furiously. It was not the sort of thing he could condone. Once he had even been tempted to fire Montgomery because his subordinate had allowed – even encouraged – his soldiers to use controlled brothels in France. Still, he could see the ex-Premier's reasoning. He was determined to save the regiment in which his son had once briefly served and he would use any means at his disposal to do so. "It's not for me to comment on the morality of this matter, sir," he said frostily at last. "Those are not methods I would use myself. But I *do* agree with your reasoning. All these American generals from Eisenhower downwards have been created by their own publicity. Now they have become addicted to it, and they can be victims of their own publicity as well. What is the phrase they always use: 'You've got to keep your nose clean.' There is something in what you say sir—"

He broke off, as if he were not accustomed to so much talk; or perhaps he was too embarrassed to go on about a subject which was very distasteful to him.

Churchill chuckled and took another puff at his big cigar. "I know you disapprove, Field Marshal, but these things have to be done. I think the time has come to address General Patton personally. Curious isn't it," he added, walking over to the stained glass window to stare at the brick wall that he had built with his own hands a long time before, "that the fate of the SAS now lies in the hands of an American, whom Hitler once called, I believe the 'cowboy general'."

160

Alanbrooke didn't respond. Churchill was undoubtedly a great man, he told himself. All the same he was a politico – 'a frock', as they had called them in the First War – who would stop at nothing to achieve his aims. He was glad he was a simple soldier who had managed to keep his hands clean till his retirement. "Is there anything else I can do for you, sir?" he asked, breaking the brooding silence at last.

Churchill turned and stared at him, as if he were seeing him for the first time. "Not at the moment. Please, if you would, keep me informed of any signals when they come in from the O'Sullivan group. Now I think I shall sit down and compose my thoughts." He grinned wickedly. "It is not every day that I blackmail an American senior commander . . .!"

Chapter Three

The two of them were caught completely by surprise. They had just left the hide from which they had observed the activity at the villa when they bumped straight into the sentry who had concealed himself in a grove of fir trees. Now he stepped out threateningly, Schmeisser machine-pistol tucked well into his hip and barked, "*Halt, wer da?*"

Rory's mind reacted immediately. Anyone who was fool enough to challenge them had a slow military mentality. "Scoot!" he cried and threw himself to one side of the track. Miles did the same on the other side, already grabbing for his Colt.

The blast of slugs hissed just above their heads. The noise was tremendous. The chatter of the slugs echoed and re-echoed around the circle of snow-capped mountains. Miles wrenched out his pistol and fired in the same moment. The German shrieked with pain and instinctively fired again in his death throes. The salvo went straight into sky. Next moment he pitched forward, dead before he hit the grass.

Miles jumped to his feet. "All right, Rory?" he called.

"All right," Rory called back and rose to his feet. "Come on, let's leg it, Miles!"

Followed by Miles, Rory started to hobble back

162

to their hidden jeep. But that initial burst from the Schmeisser had alerted the rest. There were shouts of alarm, cries of rage, someone began shrilling a whistle. Wild shots slashed the evening air. A man popped up to Miles' right, who fired instinctively. The big round at such short range lifted the German right off his feet then he slammed down again, falling to his knees, his bleeding face dripping on to his chest in red gore.

They ran on.

From the trees where they had concealed the jeep, Smith 175 and Joe Roseblum darted out of the foliage and, crouching low, held their Stens at the ready, on the lookout for any pursuers.

They didn't have to look long. A handful of Germans burst out of the bushes behind the two running officers. Smith 175 reacted immediately. "Try this on for frigging size," he snarled and aimed a burst between the two O'Sullivans.

It was a daring and very dangerous trick, but one which the veterans of the SAS like the big ex-Guardsman were used to. The tracer thrashed between the two running men and slammed on to the men chasing them. They stopped with startling suddenness as if they had run into a brick wall. Then they went down like ninepins, thrashing and screaming in their death agonies.

Smith wasted no more time. He flung himself behind the wheel of the jeep. "Keep at 'em Joe!" he yelled above the racket and started the jeep. Fiercely he gunned the engine so that it wouldn't stall at a crucial moment in the icy mountain air, while Joe fired controlled bursts to left and right as more Germans emerged cautiously from the trees on all sides.

Panting furiously the two officers flung themselves

into the vehicle, as Joe backed off, still firing. "Take her away, James!" Rory called with a weak attempt at humour.

Smith 175 needed no urging. The situation was getting out of hand, he told himself. As Joe flung himself into the canvas seat next to him, he let out the clutch. The jeep shot forward, bucking and spluttering with its cold engine.

A picket fence loomed up in front of them. "Hold tight!" Smith yelled and pushed his foot down hard on the accelerator. The jeep shot forward, followed by a lethal burst of fire from their pursuers. Rory O'Sullivan held his breath. If they got stuck on the fence it would be the end. Their pursuers would be on to them and he had no illusions about what would happen to them then. They would he shot out of hand. They knew too much.

At the wheel, Smith tensed. The knuckles of his hands holding it went white. The jeep struck the fence and something cracked. There was the sudden cloying stink of escaping petrol and then they were through, trailing smashed wood behind them. But even as they started to ascend the mountain road to where the others were hidden, Smith 175 had the sinking feeling that something had gone wrong. The jeep was losing speed all the time.

The cross-eyed man with the Sten gun watched the damaged jeep disappear round the bend in the mountain road and, in spite of the increasing darkness, he could see the wet patches it had left behind. He bent for a moment, dipped his finger in one of them and held the digit to his nose. It stank of petrol. He laughed. "They've ruptured the petrol tank," he announced. "They can't go far, boys! You . . . get back to the

164

villa and report to the chief. All right, the rest of you, follow me!" The chase was on again.

Now Smith was sweating heavily. He willed the failing jeep to make it up to the forest where the other jeep was hidden. He knew they were in serious trouble. The little American vehicle was losing power by the second. Behind them he could hear excited cries and calls in German. They were still being followed. "Damn and blast!" Smith 175 cursed. "Move it you bitch!"

The forest was still some 100 yards away, already wreathed in dark shadows, something for which Rory O'Sullivan was grateful. He had already reasoned that the damaged jeep was going to pack up on them. And they could only pack themselves in the second jeep with the other four with the greatest of difficulty. They would have to hide and hope for the best. "Come on Smithie!" he urged, "keep her going. Not much farther now!"

"Doing my best, sir," the big Sergeant grunted. "But the bloody cowson is slowing down all the time."

Rory made a swift decision. "All right, we'll abandon her, Smithie. Turn her round and then we're all gonna do a bunk."

Smith 175 didn't ask questions. With a jerk of the steering wheel, he spun the jeep round. Then he dropped from behind the wheel, leaving the brake off and the gear in neutral. Hastily the others abandoned the damaged vehicle too, as Smith ran to the back and with a deep grunt gave a hefty push. The jeep started to roll down back the track as the four of them scampered for the cover of the firs.

As the first of their pursuers came running round the bend, the runaway jeep smashed right into them, bowling them over. Immediately wild, confused firing broke out as the Germans were caught completely off guard. The fugitives used the respite to their advantage. Hurriedly they piled into the other jeep with Joe and Smith perched on the bonnet, there was no other space.

Tashy Kennedy set off, peering between the two of them, ducking instinctively as the branches lashed the front of the vehicle. Behind them they could hear wild, angry shouts and the sound of engines. The pursuers had taken up the chase once more.

Desperately, Rory O'Sullivan tried to figure a way out. They were climbing steeply now, the engine labouring under the strain of carrying eight men up such a sharp incline. Ahead of them loomed the rocky slopes above the tree line. He had to find cover for his team soon. Out there on the naked rocky slope they would be sitting ducks until darkness fell and hid them.

Whoosh! Rory O'Sullivan flashed a look upwards in the same instant that the flare exploded in a burst of brilliant, incandescent white light. Their pursuers were trying to pinpoint them in the green waste of the fir forest.

"Frig this for a game of soldiers!" Corporal Stevens cursed and balancing himself the best he could in the swaying jeep he pulled the pin out of a .36 grenade and flung it behind him with all his strength. It hit the ground, bounced, rolled a few more feet, then exploded in a blast of violent scarlet flame. In that same instant half a dozen of their pursuers broke out of the trees straight into the blast.

Men went down on all sides, screaming in agony. One of them clawed at the air, as if determined to stay upright like a man climbing the rungs of a ladder. To no avail; his knees crumpled weakly and he went down, gasping for air, to die a moment later.

"Good show!" Rory called, still trying to make his mind up what to do next. Now it seemed that the whole slope was swarming with armed Germans. He could heard them shouting to each other, bellowing orders and asking for directions the way they had always done in an attack during the war. Perhaps they thought the amount of noise would frighten their enemies.

Suddenly, next to him, Miles cried, "Look at that gully, Rory." He jerked at his uncle's arm to attract his attention. "What about that?"

Rory flashed a look at the rocky entrance to a sort of narrow valley, with the trees grouped tightly on both sides. "Do you think we could get the jeep in there, Miles?" he asked, as the sounds behind them increased once more, indicating that their pursuers hadn't given up. They were following the sound the overworked jeep's engine was making.

"We can try!" Miles shouted back.

At the wheel, Tashy Kennedy acted at once. He spun the wheel round, as Rory ordered, "Everyone out! Lighten the load. Come on, at the double! There's no time to be wasted."

They needed no urging. Their pursuers were getting close again. As one they dropped over both sides of the little jeep. Now relieved of the weight of seven men, the engine picked up. Quickly, Kennedy took his foot off the accelerator. In first gear he advanced into the green gloom, hearing and feeling the sides of the jeep scraping against the rock wall. Tashy bit his bottom lip with tension. His hands guiding the wheel were hot and wet with sweat. "Come on!" he grunted to himself. "Come on, yer bugger – *make it*!"

Then his heart suddenly skipped a beat. The jeep had snagged somewhere. It had stopped moving. Behind, the sounds of their pursuers were getting louder and louder as they crashed through the firs, shouting to each other all the time.

Rory saw the problem at once. The jeep was stuck. "Come on, chaps, lend a hand!"

Together they pushed and strained, while Tashy revved the engine crazily. The shouts were getting ever closer now. In a matter of minutes they would be discovered. Then with a great gasp of relief they relaxed as the jeep started to move once more. A moment later it had disappeared into the gully and they were all frantically brushing away the signs of its passing with branches torn from the trees before disappearing themselves into the green gloom.

Then they crouched there in the chill darkness, fingers curled around the triggers of their weapons, nerves tingling as they listened to the sounds of the hunters all about them, crashing through the trees, obviously wondering where the jeep had gone.

Next to Rory, Joe Rosenblum, whispered tensely into the officer's ear, "They can't figure how the jeep has got away. One of them, I think it must be their boss, the cross-eyed geezer, keeps ordering them to shut up and listen for the sound of the motor. But of course there isn't any."

Rory nodded and said nothing. He was too tense. Desperately, he willed them to go away so that he could make their next move. The chasers seemed, however, to hang around for ages higher up the gully. Night had already descended. Now he could catch the glimpses of their torches as they flashed them in the undergrowth, trying to find the SAS troopers.

But in the end, after what seemed an eternity, their followers started to move down the mountainside again towards the villa and Joe whispered in Rory's ear, "One of them is saying he thinks we've done a complete bunk." He breathed out hard. "Thank God for that!"

Finally the sounds died out altogether, to be replaced by the hush of the night wind. Stevens, crouched next to Tashy Kennedy, whispered, "Tashy, I thought I was gonna piss mesen back there."

"*Thought*," Tashy echoed. "I bloody well did . . .!"

Chapter Four

Patton came out of the office where the red scrambler phone was, flushed with rage, his pooch following him, its sawn-off tail between its legs, as if it were ashamed of being English. He slapped his riding crop against his boots and said to his aide, Colonel Codman: "Do you know who that was on the scrambler just then?"

Charles Codman shook his head. "No General, I don't."

"It was Winnie of all people."

"You mean Mr Churchill?" Charles Codman asked incredulously.

"Yes, goddamit, I do," Patton snapped and flopped down in his chair. "Pass me the bourbon, Charlie. I need a stiff frigging drink!"

His aide did as was requested and wondered what the ex-British premier was doing calling Patton in remotest Bavaria. Patton let him wait, while he sipped the large drink in smouldering silence.

Finally, Patton said, "I thought it was just a social call at first. You know what the limeys are like. They make all this frigging small talk at first before they get round to talking turkey. He asked me what I thought of the situation, how my relations were with the Mongolians. I told him frigging awful. He laughed at that. Then completely out of the blue he asked me about Ruth!"

170

Codman looked at his boss, startled. "Ruth!" he echoed. "Ruth Gordon?"

"Exactly."

"Your niece?"

"Oh for chrissake, Charlie! You know I'm fucking her. Have been since she was a kid back in the '30's. So why does Churchill ask about her 'good health', as he fucking well phrased it. You know as well as I do, he was trying to put the screws on me."

"How?"

"Well," Patton's skinny face was suddenly bitter, "he hinted he was going to talk to Ike in Frankfurt later on and everybody knows that Ike is more limey than the limeys and that he's running for frigging president. What was the undertone? I'll spell it out for you, Charlie. Talk turkey with me, General Patton, or I might just well happen to mention your relationship with Ruth to Ike. And as you will know, Charlie, I've been on Ike's shit list for a long time now. He's just looking for an excuse to remove me from command of the Third Army."

Codman frowned. His master didn't know when he should keep his big mouth shut. He was always talking out of turn. Somehow Codman knew that it would all end badly for General 'Blood an' Guts' Patton. "But what did Churchill want from you, General?" he asked.

Patton lit one of those huge cigars of his which his doctors had forbidden him to smoke, but then he didn't give a damn about doctors. He had failed to die in battle during the war, as he had always wanted. Now, doctors meant nothing to him. He just wanted to die and have done with it. He pointed the cigar at Codman like an offensive weapon and answered, "Charlie, the old limey fart says there is something very fishy going

171

on in the Third Army area. According to him there is a team from the English Army in our area trying to pick up a wanted war criminal; apparently he tortured some limeys during the war, something like that. It's quite illegal according to Winnie." He flushed an even darker red. "And it sure as hell is. I didn't give my permission for them to come in here. But no matter. He wants me to help that team because apparently there are bigger issues involved and I think Winnie is right there for once. You remember that Kraut gold thing I mentioned to Ziller?"

Codman nodded. "Yes, General."

"Well, that's involved us, according to Winnie, and so I think we're gonna have to do something because if Ike finds out that I'm letting the Krauts get away with stashing their loot in Switzerland or somewhere, he's got me by the nuts. Yeah, my nuts would sure be in the wringer and Ike wouldn't like anything better than that," he added bitterly. "Now I've won the war for him, he don't need me any more."

Codman knew what his superior meant. Patton felt that he had pulled the chestnuts out of the fire for Eisenhower, especially the previous December when the great German surprise attack had taken place in the Ardennes. Now Ike thought of Patton as an embarrassment and the sooner the latter went the better for Ike. "So what are you going to do, General?" he asked.

"I'll have to get on to it. I want Ziller to offer some protection to these limeys Winnie mentioned. At the same time I want Ziller to get on the stick and find out what the frig's going on with this Nazi gold. I don't want Ike's kikes in Frankfurt poking their long kike noses into it."

Codman caught himself just in time from telling the

172

General not to use that word 'kike'. But he knew it wouldn't do any good anyway. Patton said what he thought and disliked without any caution these days. Perhaps he had a death wish.

"Do you want me to contact Colonel Ziller?" he asked instead, realising as he glanced at his wrist-watch that it was long after office hours. "It might be a little difficult."

"No sweat. He's got a goddam duty officer, hasn't he? Besides, you know my tame Kraut, he's always on frigging duty . . ."

But for once General Patton was wrong. His 'tame Kraut' had decided he needed some relaxation after the events of the day at the villa and the shoot-out with the mysterious English who had seemingly vanished into thin air.

Now Ziller lay on the couch of the living room in his own villa, with his slacks down around his ankles, while the girl got ready for him.

She was pretty in the hefty Bavarian fashion, with big hands that looked capable of carrying five or six litres of beer at one go. There were a lot of peasant girls like that. It was for that reason he had brought the jar of vaseline from the bathroom and had ordered her to rub some on the palms of her hands, which had puzzled her greatly. He had enlightened her about his needs and she had looked at him rather strangely, but she was carrying out his wishes, talking to herself about how funny the '*Amis*' were.

"Are you ready?" he cut her short finally.

"Yes sir," she answered looking at her greased palms in a slightly bewildered fashion.

"Good," he ordered curtly, "then you can begin. Firm but not too hard, do you understand?"

"Yes sir," she answered and knelt awkwardly between his legs while he lay back and attempted to relax, though his mind was still buzzing with the events of the day.

She began a little hesitantly, staring at his flaccid sexual organ as if she didn't quite know how to go about it. It was obvious she hadn't done anything like this before for a man. Tentatively she put her big hand on it and gave it a slight tug.

"Not so gently," he ordered, closing his eyes and allowing his imagination to wander. Once he had been married and had done other things. But now he had been reduced to this and he knew one had to have a powerful imagination to make it work.

"Yes, sir," she said dutifully and tugged harder.

"That's better," he sighed and started to think of fleshy thighs, clad in black sheer silk stockings and knickers. That usually did it.

She began to pull very vigorously. That and his imagination began to do the trick. He started to harden. Once it was all over, he told himself, he would have a good wash down there, take a stiff drink and then go to bed and sleep like an angel.

But that wasn't to be. Suddenly the telephone next to the couch began to ring. For a moment he told himself to ignore it. Then his strict sense of Prussian discipline took over.

"One moment!" he commanded.

The woman stopped immediately. She was glad to. Men, real men, didn't behave like this, she told herself. Perhaps she'd take off her knickers and show him it. That might speed things up. This way was going to take time and she had two children back home she had to feed before they went to bed or they'd be up half the night moaning that they were hungry, which was true.

174

All they had eaten this day was cabbage soup, watery and meatless, with a hunk of dry bread.

Ziller picked up the phone. "Colonel Ziller here!" he snapped.

"Ziller!"

The Colonel started. There was no mistaking that squeaky, high-pitched voice. It was Patton.

"General, sir," he gasped. "How can I help?" It was a foolish statement to make to anyone like Patton. But he had been so surprised that he couldn't think of anything else to say.

"Ziller," Patton was saying, "there's something going on at your neck of the woods. I want you to get on the stick and do something about it pretty damned tootsweet!"

"What, sir?" Ziller asked, though already he felt he knew what the fiery Third Army Commander meant.

"This. I have information from another source, Ziller, that it's got something to do with the Kraut gold, and that our own people are involved. Yes," Patton added bitterly, "our own guys on the take working together with the Krauts. God, what a world!"

"But sir," Ziller said, "where do I start?"

"*Start?*" Patton shouted. "What kind of crap is that! Buddy, you'd better get off yer keester and start earning your pay or those colonel's eagles will vanish from your shoulders pretty damn quick. Is that clear, Ziller?"

"Yes sir," Ziller answered miserably as the phone was slammed down at the other end in Bad Toelz.

For what seemed an eternity Ziller slumped there in a very un-Prussian posture, his mind reeling. What was he going to do? Obviously the net was closing in. It could be only a matter of days, perhaps even hours now. Instinctively he knew that Patton's source was those mysterious Englishmen who had vanished

175

completely. For all he knew they were still watching the villa waiting for the blind one's next move. Then they would jump into action, and again Blood an' Guts would get in on the act.

The woman was waiting, but Ziller forgot his own needs. He indicated the cigarettes on the little table and said thickly, "Take 20 and go. I won't need you now after all. I have work to do."

The woman picked up the cigarettes and stuffed them into her pocket. She curtsied and left. The cigarettes represented a small fortune on the black market. The kids would have fried eggs and potatoes this night. That would stop their whining.

Ziller didn't even notice her go. He considered for a while, knowing whatever decision he made now would probably end his career in the military. It would mean, too, that he would not be able to go back to the States for a long time, perhaps even for ever. So that there had to be dough, plenty of it for him, so that he could take on a new identity in some country a long way away from Europe and a country with which the United States had no extradition treaty.

With a hand that trembled slightly he picked up the phone, knowing even as he did so that the die had been cast. Once he spoke to the blind one to warn him, there would be no going back.

Dieter answered. He said in that affected falsetto of his, "Yes, can I help you?"

"It's me," Ziller answered, still having sense enough not to use his name over the telephone system in case the snoopers from Frankfurt were tapping the line.

"Yes?"

"You'd better connect me with the chief. Something has gone wrong – very seriously wrong, in fact."

176

Chapter Five

"They're going to do a bunk," Miles said, "I'm sure of that, Rory."

They huddled in the freezing green gloom of the gully, spooning cold Meat and Veg compo rations out of the tins, listening to all the activity below, occasionally catching glimpses of lights as trucks came and went.

Rory crumbled a piece of hardtack into the horrid mess in his tin, took a spoonful because he knew he had to eat something against the cold wind blowing in from the snow-capped peaks above them, and said, "You're right. Somehow I feel that we've set the cat among the pigeons."

It was about then that Smith 175, who had been sent out on a lone patrol to watch the activity below at the villa, came back into the gully, whispering carefully as he did so, "It's me. Sergeant Smith." He knew his SAS. At moments of danger they shot first and asked questions afterwards.

Rory handed him the jug of GS Quartermaster's run which he had been handing out generously to the men once darkness had fallen and the cold had seemed to eat into their very bones. "Have a gargle first, Smithy," he ordered.

"Ta, Boss," the big ex-Guardsman said gratefully and tilting the jug took a hefty swig, belched and commented as he felt the fiery liquid slam into his stomach, "That's just what the doctor ordered!"

Rory waited another moment, then he asked, "Well, Smithy?"

"They've got the wind-up by the looks of it, Boss. They're ready to do a runner. Trucks are coming and going all the time, all driven by them Yankee darkies. The Jerries are loading them up with something heavy. They're panting and groaning as if they're real knackered under the weight."

Rory looked significantly at Miles in the green darkness. Miles nodded his understanding. "Bullion, gold bullion," he commented.

"I should think so. And that bastard Dr Barsch?" Rory asked the Sergeant, as the moon scudded from behind the clouds and illuminated the mountainside for the first time, casting its spectral light down the valley to the villa below.

"He's out there with the Jerries, Boss," the big NCO answered.

Rory's blue eyes shone dangerously and Smith 175 said hurriedly, "There's armed Jerries everywhere. We've alerted them, I think. I'm sure they're on the lookout for us."

Rory tugged the end of his nose and absorbed the information. Finally he asked, "How many of them do you think there are, Smithie?"

Smith didn't even consider. "Too bloody many of 'em, Boss," he snorted. "Must be at least a hundred of 'em, counting the darkies."

Miles looked worried in the silver light of the moon.

Rory thought and then said, "Our first task is to get Barsch. That's what we've come all this way for.

We've got to take our revenge for the sake of our dead comrades."

There was a subdued murmur of agreement from the others.

"All the same, there's something big going on here as well, which has to be stopped. Yanks working in the pay of Jerries and armed Huns running around all over the place. We can't let them get away with that."

"Why not try to get some help from the Yanks themselves, Boss? I mean I know the Yanks are not much cop as soldiers. But if there's enough of 'em . . ." Tashy Kennedy suggested.

"I'm afraid by the time we've gone through channels and got help from the Yanks the birds will have flown the coop," Rory answered. "We've got to deal with this bad business ourselves and tonight or early tomorrow morning."

"Sir?"

"Yes, Stevens," Rory said. "What is it?"

"An idea," the young, handsome soldier said a little hesitantly, for he was the youngest of the veterans apart from Miles O'Sullivan.

"Piss or get off the pot," Smith 175 urged. "We ain't got all night, yer know."

"I know, Sarge," Stevens answered. "But I thought if we can hold 'em up when they're about to leave, we can fix that bastard Barsch and then scoot. If we can make enough noise the Yanks down in Garmisch would have to come out here and investigate. Then the balloon would go up and it would be up to the Yanks to sort it out."

Rory absorbed the other man's suggestion for a few moments before saying, "It sounds a good idea, Corp. But how are we going to hold them up? And remember we've only got one jeep left for the lot of us. It's going to be a bit difficult with one jeep to do a shoot-and-scoot op." As he said the words, he remembered old Colonel Paddy* snorting, "It's got to be in like Flynn," he had meant Errol Flynn, the film actor and his reputation as a lightning seducer, "that's what a shoot-and-scoot op's all about."

"Sir," Stevens said a little hesitantly. "We could use the jeep to block the exit road from the villa on to the main road to Garmisch."

"Well, that would hold things up for a bit," Rory agreed. "But that's about it."

"Yes, but if the jeep was prepared," Stevens said significantly, "they could be in for a little surprise. Then we could do this Barsch bloke and run for it. The Yanks could deal with the rest."

"*Prepared?*" Rory echoed, puzzled.

"Yes sir. We've got grenades . . . we've got plenty of petrol," Stevens answered with more confidence now. "I reckon we could do quite a bit of damage before we run for it, and the Yanks wouldn't be able to ignore what's going on at the villa."

Miles O'Sullivan whistled softly. "I see what you're getting at, Corp," he said, and next to him Tashy Kennedy said irreverently, "As the actress said to the bishop."

"All right, Corp," Rory O'Sullivan followed, warming to the idea by the second, "let's hear more . . ."

*   *   *

* Colonel Paddy Mayne, his former regimental commander. See John Kerrigan: *Surprise Attack*, for further details.

Down at the villa all was hectic activity. Ever since Ziller's warning, men had been bustling back and forth loading the bullion on to the trucks of the black transportation company which Ziller had bought for this operation. The blacks, mostly illiterate farmhands from the South, who had once worked for the 'Red Ball Express' during the war, didn't really know what it was all about, but the promise of $500 for each one of them at the end of the operation had done the trick. As one of them, a big hulking sergeant, had expressed it to Ziller, "Colonel, suh, I'd carve up my dear old ma for that kinda dough!"

In the porch of the villa, Barsch, nervous and knowing that somehow he had to get out of this operation while he was still alive, briefed Ziller on the route they should take. For his part, Ziller was equally as nervous. He, too, didn't trust the blind one and especially his effeminate boy friend Dieter. All he wanted was to get his hands on a great number of greenbacks and get out from under. The blind one made promises, lots of them, but he didn't trust him or his promises. Now that Patton had got into the picture it was going to be every man for himself.

Ziller listened and said, "We'll move out just after midnight, I think. The white mice," he meant the American MPs, "usually go to ground then. The curfew's in force and there's not much traffic about, so they get some shut-eye till their shift ends."

Barsch nodded without interest. He, too, like Ziller was currently thinking how he could get his hands on some foreign currency, preferably American dollars, and then hide once more. This operation was destined for trouble, he knew it in his bones.

"How are we getting on, gentlemen?" a gentle yet sinister voice enquired.

The two of them turned, startled. It was Dieter, grinning at them from the doorway in his crooked fashion as if he enjoyed startling people, which he did.

Hurriedly Ziller told him what had been planned and the homosexual nodded his approval. "Yes, that sounds realistic. It means that we should be in France by mid-morning tomorrow. Twelve hours later and we shall be crossing the Swiss frontier. Then," he threw up his hands in an expansive gesture for him, "we shall simply play U-boats" – he meant disappear – "until the time comes for us to make our re-appearance."

Barsch made the appropriate noises and Ziller said, "I worry only about those damned Englishmen who have disappeared. They can prove difficult, especially if they go to the American authorities."

Dieter gave him his cold, calculating smile and said, "My dear *Oberst* Ziller, you need have no fears! We shall be on our way long before the Tommies can do something. After all, everyone knows the Tommies spend most of their time drinking tea. It will take them an age to get anything done, eh."

Ziller wasn't convinced, but he said nothing. Barsch excused himself and went hurriedly inside the villa. He had seen where Dieter had hidden his pistols. While the former was talking to the *Ami* he would steal one of them. It would give him the kind of insurance he felt he needed, for, like Ziller, he didn't share the 'warm brother's' overweening confidence. He had survived the war by using his wits and thinking things out in advance. He was going to survive the peace in the same way.

Up above the villa, the handful of SAS troopers also prepared for what was to come. Under the direction of Rory O'Sullivan they filled the tanks of the remaining jeep right up to the brims. The remaining jerricans of petrol were opened and a little of their contents was poured away. Now they, too, were ready for what was to come.

"Matches and lavatory paper?" Rory enquired.

"I've got the matches, Boss," Smith 175 answered.

"And I've got the arse paper," Tashy Kennedy added. "Never could stand the issue army form blank." He was referring to the khaki-coloured square of rough toilet paper which came with the compo rations. "Brought me own roll with me." He held up a roll of bright pink paper. "Cost a couple of bob, as well!"

Rory chuckled and Corporal Stevens said in an affected voice, "Oh, hain't we posh! Yer'll be drinking yer char with yer little pinkie up and out soon, Tashy!"

Tashy stuck up his middle finger by way of a reply.

"All right," Rory cut into the banter. "We're ready to start! Smith, you take charge of the driving. But don't start up, we can coast down. The track's steep enough. We don't want to alert them before they're ready to take off. We want them all bunched in a convoy when the balloon goes up. With a bit of luck on our side, there'll be mass confusion." He paused and looked around at their faces, all serious and set now in the hard, silver light of the room. "Remember this. One thing we *must* do. There can be no failure on this."

They waited expectantly as he let his warning sink in. Then Rory said, his voice harsh and grating, "If it's the last thing we do, we've got get that bastard Barsch. All right, let's move out . . ."

Chapter Six

Down below, bathed in the silver light of the midnight moon, Garmisch was silent. Even the drunken GIs had staggered back to their barracks, urged on by club-wielding MPs. As for the Germans they huddled beneath their thick *federdecken*, stomachs rumbling with hunger, and tried to sleep in the bitter night cold. The world, it seemed, had gone to sleep.

But not in the villa.

Here the hectic activity continued, as *Der Blinde* prepared the convoy to move out on its way to the safety and future of Switzerland. "Don't worry," he reassured Dieter more than once with a tender pressure on those soft hands, "we shall return! Germany will be great yet once again. This is still Germany's century, my dearest."

Back and forth the sweating blacks went, staggering under the weight of the crates of gold bullion, watched suspiciously all the time by the armed German civilians under the command of the cross-eyed man. Barsch kept out of the way, as did Ziller. But both of them had their eyes on truck No. 3, a typical US 'deuce and a half', as the blacks called it, which contained the foreign currency. If they were going to flee with money to keep them for the rest of their lives, No. 3 was the truck which they needed. Dieter, as sharp-eyed as ever, saw the looks on

184

their faces as they watched the truck being loaded and knew instinctively what they were thinking and what they intended. He gripped the Walther pistol concealed in his right pocket more tightly and grinned to himself. They'd be dead men, he told himself, before they could lay a finger on the money in No. 3 truck.

Now they were almost ready. Dieter strode over to the blind one. "We shall take the middle vehicle," he said. "I think that's wiser."

Der Blinde didn't object. "Anything you say, Dieter," he said. "You are my right hand, as you know. If anything should happen to me, you're in charge. After all you are young. You are Germany's future." Not caring whether or not any of the blacks were watching, he reached up and dragging Dieter's blond head down gently, kissed him on the lips.

Watching them embrace so openly, Ziller felt like spitting in disgust. What perverts they were, he told himself. And he had been fool enough to believe that perverts like that could be the architects of the New Germany! Now it was too late. All he could do was save himself while there was still time.

Outside, the cross-eyed man called, "*Los* . . .! *Los*! Mount up!" Then in heavily accented English, "Drivers, you will start your engines . . . pliz!"

Hastily the blacks swung into their seats, each one accompanied by an armed guard. Dieter was taking no chances.

He helped the blind one to the middle truck. Then seating himself safely next to the driver and the armed guard, he hung out on the mud-guard and yelled, "*Wir fahren!*"

The drivers revved their engines and the night air was suddenly full of the cloying stink of petrol. The drivers thrust home first gear. In his seat, *Der Blinde* started to sing softly that old song of his youth when he had been full of hope and enthusiasm: "*Die Fahne hoch . . . die Reihen fest geschlossen . . . SA marschiert . . .!*"*

The young black driver looked sideways at the old Kraut singing a song he knew nothing about, though once it had brought fear and trembling to the enemies of Nazi Germany. Still it was no concern of his what the old fart did. All he was concerned with was the dough they were going to pay him at the end of this trip. Leroy let out the clutch and the truck lurched forward.

Now the whole convoy, lights still dimmed as in wartime, began to move up the trail to the country road that led out of Garmisch and on to the West. Dieter swung himself inside the truck once more and announced, "This is it! This day will go down in the history books as the one which marked the start of Germany's Fourth Reich!"

Der Blinde stopped singing and exclaimed, "Well said, Dieter! That it will!"

In first gear, the trucks, with their heavy loads of bullion, growled up the track keeping well to the right, for the path was small and there was a sheer drop on the left.

In the middle truck the blind one started singing again and after a while both Dieter and the armed guard joined in, singing lustily, while Leroy told himself that he'd always known that white folk were crazy, but these Krauts were the craziest of them all.

In the third truck, Colonel Ziller and Barsch looked at each other in the green light reflected from the

* The Nazi marching song: '*Das Horst Wessellied*'.

dashboard instruments. It was as if both of them knew what was going on in the other's mind. Then suddenly Ziller said in German, which he knew the black driver wouldn't understand, "When do you think it would be safest to leave the convoy?" It was a clear statement of his intentions.

Barsch knew it. His pudgy bespectacled face lit up. He had found an ally, a powerful one. "As soon as we cross from Germany into Neuf Brisach in France. I know the area well. There are people there who owe me favours, if you understand," he lowered his voice significantly.

Ziller knew well what he meant. The fat German *Herr Doktor* meant those who had collaborated with the German police authorities during the war and had now gone underground. "Go on," he urged.

"With their assistance we could go up into the High Vosges for the winter, to the German-speaking area. We could lie up there – at a price – until it was safe for us to re-surface and go—"

"To South America perhaps?" Ziller prompted, the plan already beginning to unfurl in his mind, as if it had been there all the while.

"Exactly," Barsch agreed and added, looking at the driver, "But we'll need foreign currency, plenty of it."

"That can be taken care of, *Herr Doktor*," Ziller said and tapped his leather pistol holster significantly.

Barsch nodded his understanding. Then the two of them fell silent in the green-glowing gloom, each man wrapped in a cocoon of his own thoughts and plans.

They were now almost to the height where the track joined the road leading out of Garmisch. The only sound was that of the laboured engines and the chill Alpine wind in the firs. Dieter told himself that it was

187

good they were going at last. Soon it would begin to snow, it always started snowing earlier in Bavaria than in the rest of Germany, and their journey would have been made much more difficult. He pressed the blind one's knee, reassuringly, indicating that all was going smoothly.

In a sleepy voice, the blind one, perhaps worn out from the singing of that old Nazi marching song, said, "Yes, Dieter, everything's going well, I know. Nothing can stop us now." He yawned.

Dieter sat back and tried to make himself more comfortable on the hard seat. He was tempted to close his eyes and doze off, but he thought better of it. Someone had to be charge until they were speeding out on to the main road. He yawned, probably in sympathy with the blind one's yawn. For an instant his eyes closed involuntarily.

Next moment they flashed open in alarm. Suddenly, things were beginning to happen! Up front where the track started to broaden before it reached the main road, a jeep, its lights blazing, was bearing down on them. In the back a dark figure, starkly silhouetted against the lights, was balancing, firing a tommy-gun.

The black driver shrieked as the windscreen in front of him shattered into a gleaming spider's web of broken glass. He flung up his hands in front of his face. "Hold it!" Dieter shouted in alarm. Too late. The driver lost control. The truck slithered to the right and slammed into the rock wall in the same instant that the mysterious jeep braked to a stop, its tyres shrieking in protest as it did so. Men jumped out of the jeep, save the man behind the wheel. Dieter whipped out his pistol, then with his free hand he gave the blind one a push and sent him tumbling out of the shattered door.

Not a moment too soon. Again a burst of tommy-gun fire raked the cab. The driver slumped over the wheel, dead or dying. Dieter gasped as something like a red-hot poker was thrust into his right side. He had been hit. He tumbled out of the cab too, firing as he dropped to the ground. He heard the jeep's windscreen shatter, but the driver still crouching low was gunning his engine and there were dark figures in the drainage ditch to the left, firing as well.

Dieter grabbed the blind one's arm, "Come on, it'll be all right!" he yelled. "There's only a handful of them. We'll be all right." He tugged hard and hauled the older man to his feet. Firing and holding '*Der Blinde*' protectively, he hurried back to where the second truck was beginning to slow. "Keep moving! Make the black bastard keep going!" he urged the armed German in the cab next to the terrified soldier driver.

The guard needed no urging. He jammed his automatic into the driver's skinny ribs and said threateningly, "Move ze truck! *Oder?*"

Cautiously, his dark face glistening with sweat, the driver started to edge his 'deuce and a half' around the first wrecked truck. But not for long. The man in the jeep swung the wheel expertly round and moved straight into the path of the second truck.

The jeep slammed into the bonnet of the big truck and the driver flung himself into the ditch in a shallow dive. Crouched there, Dieter could see what looked like a toilet roll being unwound from the back to where their unknown attackers were crouched in the ditch. "What in three devils' name?" he exclaimed. But he never finished. There was the blue burst of a match being lit. Abruptly his nostrils were assailed by the sickly stench of escaping petrol. The paper caught fire

189

and the flames ran the length of the paper which led into the open fuel-cap of the jeep.

"Oh my God!" Dieter yelled.

"What's going on Dieter?" *Der Blinde* began.

An angry flash, followed a second later by a blinding light as the petrol tank exploded, drowned the rest of his words.

In an instant the second truck was blazing furiously, the two men in the cab wreathed in blue flames, screaming and shrieking as fire ate at their bodies.

"Things are getting noisy!" Rory O'Sullivan yelled above the angry snap and crackle of the wild firing which had now broken out, using the old SAS phrase for the outbreak of firing. "Come on, lads! Let's seal 'em off."

Hurriedly they cut down the drainage ditch, past the stalled convoy as slugs slashed the air lethally all around them. But the defenders were much too confused to aim accurately and as soon as they had left the area of the two furiously burning trucks they were just black shadows slipping by almost noiselessly.

In truck No. 3, Barsch looked at Ziller in horror. The other man's hard face was like granite in the light that came from the blaze. He, too, was at a loss. "What are we going to do?" Barsch gasped.

Ziller made a quick decision. "Keep the driver covered. We're going to grab as many of those greenbacks as we can carry and then make a run for it. This racket is bound to bring the MPs up from Garmisch." As Barsch brought out the stolen pistol and levelled it at the bewildered young driver, Ziller grabbed at the canvas and began attempting to smash into a crate containing dollars.

Panting hard with the effort, Rory skidded to a halt

190

parallel with the last truck of the convoy. The others did the same, already reaching for the grenades inside the pockets of their camouflaged smocks. "All right," Rory yelled, "all together!"

They tugged out the pins as Rory counted off the seconds, "*ONE . . . TWO . . . THREE . . . NOW!*"

The grenades sailed through the air. Not one missed its target. The truck was racked by a series of explosions. Its back axle cracked and the rear tyres flew away. A moment later it was being seared by a terrible flame like that of a giant blowtorch. They had trapped the convoy for good.

"All right," Rory yelled above the angry crackle of small arms fire and the hiss and roar of the greedy flames. "Now let's get Barsch." From down below came the first thin wail of a police siren.

Garmisch had been alarmed.

Chapter Seven

"What the Sam Hill's going on down there, eh?" the harsh American voice demanded from the loud hailer.

Dieter, his face creased with pain, stared upwards at the road, as the spot flashed on and swept the stalled convoy with the three trucks still burning, giving away their positions only too clearly.

A white-painted jeep was stopped there, engine throbbing impatiently. Behind it there were three white half-tracks, all filled with helmeted American military policemen.

"What is it?" the blind one demanded in bewilderment.

"White mice," Dieter said, trying to conceal the pain in his voice. He didn't want *Der Blinde* to know he had been hurt, the man would go to pieces if he did, he knew that.

"What are you going to do?"

"Thus," Dieter snapped. He took careful aim, sighting on the harsh white light of the spot's beam. He pulled the trigger and the Luger exploded in his hand. There was a curse. A tinkle of glass. Abruptly the light went out.

Almost immediately the firing commenced once more as the MPs scattered from their half-tracks and, crouching or kneeling on the road, began blasting away wildly with their tommy-guns and pistols. Down below, the cross-eyed civilian's men began to return their fire.

Barsch looked wildly at Ziller as he returned, stuffing great bundles of dollar bills into his pockets. His fear was all too obvious. "What are we going to do?"

"Run for it," Ziller answered. "In this confusion we've got a good chance of getting away. And don't worry about wheels. By the time they've figured out that I'm involved in this business we'll find a vehicle in Garmisch. I've still got influence. Leave it to me. Just you get us into those French mountains, then it'll be plain sailing." He nodded at the black driver who was staring at the two of them in mystified horror. "Get rid of him. Liquidate the black bastard!"

Barsch swallowed hard, but he knew this was a test for him. The big US Colonel was ensuring that he'd do what he was ordered to do. He'd be involved one hundred per cent if he shot the driver.

"Go on," Ziller urged impatiently. "We haven't got all night if we're gonna make it." He ducked as a salvo of slugs ripped the length of the canvas where he was standing.

Barsch raised his pistol.

The driver cowered. He took his hands off the wheel. "What you gonna do, Cap'n?" he quavered.

Barsch felt like closing his eyes, but he knew he couldn't do that. He pressed the trigger for first pressure. The driver's face turned a sickly greenish colour. He raised his hands in front of his face as if he could ward off the bullet. Barsch swallowed and took second pressure. The pistol roared in his hand and the black's face disappeared in a welter of blood.

Shattered bone gleamed like polished ivory in the red, slimy gore. Without even a groan he slumped dead over the wheel.

"Come on!" Ziller cried above the racket outside. "Let's go while there's a still a chance. Down the drainage ditch . . . back to the villa."

Together they dropped in and started working their way down the slope as the slugs zipped back and forth with lethal intensity. Men were going down everywhere, writhing as they died. The pair took no notice, their only concern was to save their own skins.

The moon came out again, scudding from behind a cloud. Ziller caught a glimpse of man crouched next to a bush. He was taking no chances and fired as he ran, the angry scarlet flame stabbing the darkness. The man screamed shrilly, high and hysterical, like a woman. He reeled backwards. They ran on.

Up ahead, Rory and the rest of the SAS troopers were working their way up the stalled column, with Joe Rosenblum in front, crying in German, *"Herr Doktor Barsch – hierher . . . Herr Doktor Barsch . . .!"* It was an elementary trick, but Rory reasoned it just might work. A drowning man would clutch at straws. Perhaps Barsch would think that someone was making a special attempt to rescue him. He hoped so.

Half-way down the column another truck exploded as its engine was hit by a burst of heavy machine-gun fire from the MPs on the road, the flames from the ruptured engine spreading to the spare jerricans in the back. Blazing men fled screaming from the doomed vehicle. In their panic they stumbled over the side and went rolling in a ball of fire down the slope to lie writhing in their mortal agony in the gully below.

Der Blinde was hit just about then. Even before Dieter

could help, he fell to his knees, the blood spurting from the sudden red buttonholes stitched along the length of his skinny back. He gasped with pain as Dieter knelt down and put his good arm around the old man to support him.

"No, Dieter!" *Der Blinde* sobbed, fighting for breath, "I'm finished. . . . It's up to you now. You'll make the new Ger—" The words died on his lips. Before Dieter could do anything, the inert body tore itself free from his grasp and fell to the ground.

For a moment he stared at the dead chief and his lover, as if mesmerised. Then he heard the voice calling in German, "Dr Barsch . . . Where are you? . . . Over here . . . a friend!"

He rose immediately and shook his head like a man trying to wake from a deep sleep. His grip tightened on his pistol. There were men coming up the drainage ditch from below and even at this distance he could tell by their smell that they weren't German; it was something that *Der Blinde*, who had relied on his sense of smell a great deal, had taught him. These men smelled of good perfumed soap and Virginia cigarettes, unlike the Germans. They were the enemy all right.

A blind rage overcame him, unreasoning and deadly. He stood up, fully exposing himself in the light of the blazing truck. "Over here . . . Barsch speaking!" he called above the racket, the chatter of machine-guns, the crackle of flames. "Barsch over here!"

Joe Rosenblum turned to Rory O'Sullivan who was just behind him. "It's him, sir. Just there!"

Together they clambered out of the drainage ditch. Dieter didn't give them a chance. He pumped off a full magazine and Rosenblum slammed to the ground without even a moan, dead already. Rory yelled with

pain and went down on his knees. He saw the bright
flashes as though through a haze. There was a terrible
second blow on his shoulder. He felt sick with the shock
of the impact. A third bullet hit him and knocked him
on to his back. He lay there, his muscles watery and
without strength. He tried to collect his thoughts but
couldn't. He knew he was dying.

"Mr O'Sullivan!" he heard Smith 175 cry in total
horror. The big sergeant's voice seemed to come from
a long way. He felt himself being touched. Smith
exclaimed, "Oh my God . . .!" He fired as he crouched
there. It was the last sound that Rory O'Sullivan heard.
As he died, Dieter fell too, mortally wounded.

It was then that the heart went out of the six survivors.
In their moment of triumph, their beloved leader and
their friend little Joe Rosenblum had both been killed.
Tough Corporal Stevens was standing there numbly,
tears glinting in his eyes in the ruddy light of the flames.
Smith 175 kept muttering in a broken voice, "The
second O'Sullivan to die in action since the Regiment
was formed.* What a life . . .!"

It seemed to take an eternity before the old discipline
of the SAS returned and Miles O'Sullivan resumed
command, saying, "Come on, lads, we'll bury them
later. Let's get that bastard Barsch first. That's what
we came for!"

Once again they set off on their search, leaving the
two bodies to stare sightless at the cold, unfeeling night
sky, and already beginning to stiffen in the cold air
sweeping down from the mountains.

*   *   *

* See John Kerrigan: *Kill Rommel*, for further details.

Barsch and Ziller rose from where they had dropped when the nearest bout of firing had broken out. The men who had been calling his name and title were now moving up the column. They hadn't been spotted, but Barsch was trembling almost uncontrollably. They had been looking for *him*, there was no mistaking that.

Ziller knew it too. "What was that about?" he hissed. "Why you?"

"Something . . . something I did in the war, I think," Barsch managed to stammer. "Nothing to do with this operation . . . I was just a guide. Nothing else . . . nothing important."

Ziller frowned. He had obviously allied himself to a serious liability. All the same he needed the fat German's help to get into the mountains. He made a snap decision. String him along till they reached the Vosges and once there among a German-speaking population he would be able to fend for himself; then he'd quietly get rid of Barsch. "Come on, we've got to get out of this trap! They're already beginning to surrender up there. Listen." They cocked their heads to one side. The firing was beginning to die away and they could hear individual voices already crying, "*Nicht schiessen . . . bitte nicht schiessen . . .* Don't shoot . . .!"

"The white mice'll be coming down soon to round up the survivors. It'll be only a matter of minutes before it's all over bar the shouting. *Los.*"

Pulling himself together, Barsch followed Ziller down the track. Moments later they had vanished into the darkness. Behind them the firing died away altogether.

Five minutes later, watched carefully by the handful of SAS troopers, the beefy, angry MPs were rounding up the survivors, both American and German, pushing

197

them or kicking them if they didn't move quickly enough to where a burly, red-faced sergeant was handcuffing them. Captain O'Grady, as angry as his men, kept flashing the SAS men a look. Apparently he knew all about them. That very night an urgent message had come from Patton's HQ in Bad Toelz, signed by 'Old Blood an' Guts' personally, ordering him to find and arrest Colonel Ziller and give the limeys all possible help. And the message had ended with a warning – '*No foul ups or else!*'

Each time O'Grady looked at him, Smith 175, sombre and down at the mouth, shook his head. He was the only one who had seen Barsch on that bridge across the Rhine in what now seemed another age. But so far he hadn't been arrested.

"I knew Ziller was on the take all the time. But I didn't know the big Kraut was in this racket. Hell, there must be millions in gold in those trucks."

A negro driver was led by protesting, "I'm only a dumb Southern boy, I knows nuthin, Cap'n!"

Frustrated, O'Grady aimed a kick at him, and missed, crying, "Get ya black Southern ass over there. You're for the stockade, jailbait!"

In the end it was clear that neither Barsch nor Ziller were among the dead or the prisoners. Knowing now that the limeys had lost their commander, O'Grady said, "Don't worry fellahs, we'll get 'em. I've already thrown a cordon around Garmisch and with General Patton breathing down my back it's as much as my life's worth to let them get away. Don't worry, before the night's out they'll be behind bars or my name is not Timothy O'Grady." And with that the SAS men had to be satisfied. Sadly they went down to pick up the bodies of their dead comrades.

198

Chapter Eight

They could smell the acrid odour of charred flesh even before the two of them saw what was going on. They pushed into the darkened farmyard, with even the usual dogs not barking fiercely, as if they had been deliberately silenced. Both men gripped their pistols more firmly as they crept along the shadows cast by the wall of the old farmhouse. Now, as they got closer to the barn, from which a strange flickering light they couldn't identify was coming, they could hear the sharp hiss, a splashing and subdued voices.

Barsch looked at Ziller.

The latter shrugged, but with the muzzle of his Colt he indicated the wood-burning pre-war Opel Blitz which stood in the corner, the huge container holding the gas which propelled the vehicle on its trailer behind the Blitz, like a live thing impatient to get started.

"Wheels," he mouthed. "Our transport!"

Barsch nodded his understanding.

They cautiously crept closer to the barn, the palms of their hands damp with sweat as they gripped the pistol butts. Then they saw the source of the smell. The fleshy body of a pig hung from a strut, its head bloody and its eyes closed. On his knees in front of it a burly man with a blowtorch was busy burning the bristle from the dead creature. He ran the blue flame up and down the flesh, following it with a razor-sharp knife. Next to him a fat peasant woman in a head scarf, and with a potato sack wrapped around her waist as an apron, was stirring steaming hot blood with a stick, occasionally dropping in handfuls of barley.

"*Schwarzschlachten*," Barsch whispered as the man scraping the bristle paused and took a hefty swig from a bottle of schnapps. "Black market killing." He'd seen enough of it in the village. In the dead of night they'd give the pig to be slaughtered a hefty drink or two of schnapps to knock it out so that there'd be no noise. Then they'd slit its throat, drain the blood out to make blood sausage and then chop it up into various parts for the smoke-house and other kinds of sausage. By dawn the pig would have vanished, being prepared to sell on the black market at a later date and the authorities would be not one whit wiser.

"That's why they've got the truck," Ziller agreed. "To take it away."

As the plan started to form in his brain, Ziller watched as the peasant woman walked over to the edge of the barn, squatted, and lifting up her skirt, urinated. The man scraping the pig didn't even look up.

Ziller indicated with a jerk of his pistol that Barsch should slip to the other side of the barn and check if there was anyone else in the place. He wanted to know before he put his plan into operation.

Barsch did as he was commanded, any noise he might have made covered by the hiss of the blowtorch. He peered inside intently, searching the heap of straw at the far end in case anyone was sleeping there, as farmhands often did in Bavaria.

There was no one there. He shook his head deliberately so that the American could see quite clearly.

200

Ziller nodded that he had. He slipped off the safety on his big Colt .45 and advanced on tiptoe.

The man with the blowtorch finished his task. He put the torch out and after another drink advanced on a plain white board table on which lay half a dozen knives of various sizes. He selected one and ran its blade along the base of his broad, work-hardened thumb. It was satisfactory. Whistling softly he gently cut into the white fatty flesh. He paused and spat on his big paws, leaving the knife stuck in the pig's carcass. Then he grasped it once more and putting all his weight on it, he guided the blade down the rest of the animal's body, opening it up. Without faltering he cut out the stomach and intestines and dropped them to the floor where they steamed faintly. Heart and liver followed. Then he obviously decided he needed another drink after his exertions and walked over to where the schnapps bottle rested.

"Don't drink the shitting lot!" the peasant woman growled, still stirring the blood and barley mixture which was now beginning to thicken nicely. "Save some for a poor old woman!"

Raising the bottle to his lips, the butcher said scornfully, "Poor old woman, with all them gold coins beneath her bed—" He stopped short, a look of amazement on his broad red face, the bottle poised at his lips.

The peasant woman caught the look and turned her heard to look at the door. "Jesus Maria!" she gasped, as she recognised the uniform. "*Ami Polizei*!" She lifted her apron as if she were about to throw it over her face to blot out the sight.

Ziller jerked up his pistol threateningly. "Don't move," he said harshly, "or there'll be trouble! You," he addressed the butcher, still clutching his bottle as if petrified, "is that your truck over there?"

"*Jawohl, Herr General*," the butcher quavered.

Ziller looked over his shoulder at Barsch, but still kept his pistol trained on the two peasant black-marketeers. "We've got our transport, Barsch," he said triumphantly. "All right you two, move out in front of me. Nice and quiet now. No tricks or it'll be the worse for you!"

With the butcher in the lead, followed by the peasant woman, now busily reciting a 'Hail Mary', they moved across to the truck. Outside, all was still once more. Garmisch, it appeared, had gone to sleep. Ziller nodded his approval.

"I'll keep them covered," he said to Barsch. "You watch him, while he starts the engine. *Klar*?"

"*Klar*," Barsch answered, the relief obvious in his voice. They were going to get away with it after all.

For five minutes the driver busied himself with the complicated mechanism of the gas-powered truck. Then the ancient Opel Blitz jerked into a rattling, juddering, shaking life.

Hastily Ziller pushed the terrified woman into the back, reasoning that she wouldn't dare jump out even though she was unguarded. Now dressed in the butcher's jacket and battered old grey *Wehrmacht* peaked cap, with the tarnished *Edelweiss* of the mountain troops on it, he squeezed in next to the man, followed a moment later by Barsch.

Swiftly Ziller gave his instructions, threatening the butcher that if he did anything wrong, he wouldn't last another five minutes, to which the butcher replied in a trembling voice, "Don't worry, *Herr General*, I want to live!"

One minute later they were on their way heading for the West and freedom . . .

Smith 175 could find no peace. O'Grady, the big MP captain, elated at the success of his operation, had offered to send him and the rest back to their post in Garmisch. There they could eat and sleep and "wash up," as he phrased it, till they captured the two escapees. "And believe you me, they're not gonna get away," he had snorted. "You can bet your bottom dollar on that!"

But Smith and the others knew they wouldn't be able to sleep until it was all over and what they had come here to do was done. The veteran Smith, in particular, couldn't get over the death of Rory O'Sullivan. He remembered how he had 'deserted' from his Guards battalion in the desert to follow the first O'Sullivan into the SAS. Now the second one was dead, too. Were the O'Sullivans jinxed? But young Miles had survived at least and when this was all over, the big NCO told himself, he would be returned to his battalion and the SAS would be finished.

But now as the huddle of weary, heartbroken SAS lounged next to the main American roadblock running westwards out of Garmisch, Smith wanted revenge too. 'An eye for an eye, a tooth for a tooth,' the old refrain from his Sunday school days back in the early '30s kept going through his brain as if some inner force was attempting to drive him on to avenge his dead comrades. 'You're going barmy, Smithie,' he kept telling himself. But he knew in his heart he wasn't mad.

While the Americans at the roadblock were still excited and animated at their coup, talking about "all them greenbacks", and "did you get a gander at them gold bullion bars", the English were subdued, puffing fitfully at the Camels and Lucky Strikes the triumphant Americans had given them, grunting moodily if spoken to. Miles had tried to spark them up, without success.

Besides his own heart wasn't in it, as he thought of what the family would say when they learned of Rory's death. All of them had been soldiers at one time or another. They were used to family and friends being killed in action for the sake of the 'King-Emperor' as they always phrased it. But there weren't too many young O'Sullivans left to keep up the family's 300-year-old tradition of service to 'all that red on the map'.

Suddenly one of the Americans broke into Miles' reverie. "Something coming," he announced, cocking his head to one side in order to hear better. "Don't sound like one of ours."

"Might be a Kraut," another MP suggested.

"Curfew ain't over yet," the first man said.

"Well, it could be one of them Krauts who have permission to stay out during the curfew."

O'Grady said, "Cut the cackle, you dumb cluck! We don't want to give our position away yet. Let's wait and see, huh?" He peered into the darkness to their front and said after a moment, "It's a Kraut all right. You can see the embers from the fire. One of them crazy wood-burning trucks o' theirs. Stand by!"

The military policemen stopped their chatter, while the SAS troopers nipped their cigarettes out and put the dog-ends behind their ears. They waited as the old truck grunted and groaned its slow way towards them.

When it was almost upon them, O'Grady stepped

into the road and yelled in atrocious German, "*Halt!*
. . . *Mak schnell* . . . *Halt*, you Kraut arseholes!"

With a squeak of rusty brakes, the Opel Blitz came
slowly to a stop, giving off the smell of wood smoke.
Behind it the big tank of gas billowed in and out as
if it were having a hard job to keep going like some
ancient asthmatic in the throes of a fatal attack.

Curiously Smith 175 watched as O'Grady advanced
upon the cab, shouting above that strange, sighing
whine, "Okay, let's see some ID. *Papiere!*"

Inside Ziller dug the muzzle of his pistol into the
butcher's fat ribs. "*Los,*" he hissed, "show the *Ami*
your pass and let's get the hell out of here!"

"*Jawohl—*" the butcher began until Ziller dug the
muzzle even harder into his ribs with a curt, "None
of that *Herr General* shit!"

Next to him, Barsch started to tremble once again.
Furtively, he sought and found the door handle.
Noiselessly he started to open it.

Suspiciously, O'Grady flashed his torch into the
driver's side of the cab. "Why you out?" he demanded in
broken German. "You know curfew – *Ausgehverbot?*"

The fat butcher looked at the burly police officer
as if he might burst into tears at any moment. "*Herr
Offizier,*" he quavered, "I have pass . . . signed by the
commandant. I go to the market in Garmisch . . . food
supplies." Hastily, as if the grey document with the
shield of Shaef on the top was burning his fingers, he
handed *die Bescheinigung*, a certificate, to O'Grady.

O'Grady flashed his torch on it. He stared at the
usual pass, the kind he had seen probably a thousand
times. Then he frowned as he read the signature.
"*Zil-ler,*" he spelled out the familiar name and said
almost as if to himself, "What the Sam Hill is the

Chief of Counter-Intelligence doing signing a pass for a butch—"

In that instant Ziller fired.

O'Grady gasped with shock. His eyes grew wide and staring with disbelief. His hands fell to his stomach. Suddenly they were wet and sticky with blood. "Oh my God—" he commenced. But he never finished, instead he pitched forward and slammed into the tarmac.

"*Los!*" Ziller roared, face red and furious that they had been caught at this late stage of the game.

Barsch dropped out of the side of the ancient truck in the same moment that the terrified butcher slammed home first gear and the Blitz began to move forward, catching the MPs completely by surprise.

Not for long.

Wild firing broke out immediately. The window crumbled like soft toffee. Ziller slammed the shards of glass out with his elbow and began answering the MPs' fire. One MP went down, sighing, "Oh Christ! Why me?" Another fell over his inert body.

For once the SAS troppers reacted slowly. Then they started to unsling their weapons as Miles yelled, "It's them!"

Barsch dropped down into the ditch, unutterably grateful that all attention was concentrated on the truck. He held the money fast in his pocket, all $20,000 which Ziller had given him as a kind of a bribe. To his front there was small road bridge. Beyond that there was a thick fir wood. Once into the wood he knew he would be safe. They would need an army to comb it. He doubled forward as the wild firing continued.

Smith 175 aimed his tommy-gun as the truck slewed round. He fired from the hip and the bag of gas burst. Almost immediately a jet of blue angry flame erupted from it. The still moving truck started to cough and splutter as its power source began to decrease. Smith fired again.

Up in the cab Ziller screamed shrilly as the bullets tore his back apart. "Oh my God!" he moaned in his native German. "Oh my God . . .!"

Barsch crouched low, he was almost at the bridge now. Only a few more metres and he'd be across and deep into the wood where he'd be safe. He exerted all his energy on moving fast, the sweat dripping down his pudgy face. Into his mind flashed that time back in November 1944 when he had raced across the bridge at Kehl, seconds before the German engineers had blown it up. He had been saved then; he would be again. Luck was on his side, he knew it instinctively. The Americans were too wrapped up with the burning truck to know about him. "Yes, I'm going to do it," he chortled to himself. He'd get far away from this damned doomed Europe to some primitive country where he could live like a king on the $20,000. There, he would be able to have as many young girls as he wished. He'd—

"*Hey, you, halt!*" Smith's harsh voice cut into his frantic reverie.

Barsch kept on running. He was on the bridge now. The trees were almost within reach. By the time the man who had shouted had decided to fire he would be within the trees. Then let them find him, if they damn well could! Despite the exertion a grin appeared on his fat sweat-lathered face. Yes, they had to get up earlier in the morning to catch him! He had survived six years of war; he'd survive the next six minutes, he knew that instinctively.

As Barsch clattered over the wooden planks of the roughly repaired bridge, dodging the shell holes still visible in its superstructure, Smith gave a great gasp. "It's him!" he cried to no one in particular. "*IT'S BARSCH!*"

The fleeing man flinched at the mention of his name. It was those damned English again. They never forgot anything, blast them! He redoubled his efforts, his breath coming in great anxious gasps, his heart pounding wildly as if it might burst out of his rib-cage at any moment.

Smith flung up his tommy-gun and clicked it on to single shot. He fired. The slug whined off the iron railing of the bridge, some yard or two to Barsch's front. The fugitive saw the angry blue sparks erupt, but he wasn't afraid. He was going to do it. The firs were within grasping distance. He laughed crazily, he was indestructible! He was a born survivor. He ran on, his fat arms jerking back and forth like pistons, his eyes wild and bulging, straining to find an entrance into the wood.

Smith cursed and fired again. This time the bullet erupted just behind Barsch's flying feet, throwing up a shower of wooden splinters.

Now Barsch saw the entrance he would use – a narrow path probably made by generations of deer coming out of the wood to drink the water in the gurgling stream below: *Wildwechsel*, the locals called such paths. He'd follow it and—

He shrieked suddenly, a burning pain stabbing unbearably into his right leg. He went down on one knee, his eyes full of tears. Desperately he grabbed the iron railing and levered himself up, panting hard. Holding on to the rail, his shattered right calf jetting blood in a bright scarlet arc, he hobbled on towards the *Wildwechsel*.

Smith took careful aim and fired again. Barsch gave a great gasp as his right knee cap shattered. Desperately he tried to remain upright and moving, but his knee gave way. He sat down with a thump. He stared numbly at his shattered legs and then, almost longingly, at the path. He heard slow, solemn footsteps echoing in the hollow beneath the bridge, advancing towards him. "Help me!" he said weakly. He wasn't afraid, strangely enough. All he wanted to do was to lie down and rest. They had him, but that didn't make him fearful. They were weak and decadent, they would treat him fairly. There would be a doctor in due course, a soothing, pain-killing injection and a bed in which he could lie and rest. Oh, yes, the situation was bad, but not that bad.

The footsteps came closer, slow, steady, purposeful like those of a man who was taking his time because he was thinking hard about what to do next as he walked.

The footsteps stopped.

For a moment there was heavy silence, broken only by the crackle of the flames and his own laboured breathing. He lay there and waited. There was no pain now. He even sensed relief. They'd look after him, the fools.

"Dr Barsch?"

The query was toneless, without emotion.

"Yes, I am he," he answered in that pedantic manner which he had acquired long before when he had taught at the *Real gymnasium fur Madchen*, the Grammar School for Girls, all those virginal teenagers with their little tits and bright, innocent faces. Slowly, very slowly he turned his head and peered through his cracked pince-nez at the giant standing there in the spectral light of the sickle moon, tommy-gun clutched under his arm.

"Dr Barsch from Strasbourg?"

"Yes."

"I see," the giant said and raising his tommy-gun did something to it. Barsch, on the ground, heard the click of metal.

Still he wasn't afraid. He said primly, "Get me a doctor, will you! I am badly—" Somehow he couldn't quite remember the English word for 'wounded'. Instead he pointed at his shattered kneecap.

The giant grunted and raised the tommy-gun.

Suddenly Barsch realised his danger. Fear stabbed at his guts like the blade of a sharp knife. "What do you do?" he quavered, his careful university English now shaky.

The giant didn't answer. Instead he pressed the trigger. The machine-pistol chattered frenetically. A line of slugs ripped the length of Barsch's stomach and his guts started to slither out of the gaping wound like a grey-green snake.

"Why?" Barsch asked, gasping for breath, as the life force began to ebb from his shattered body. "*Why?*"

Smith 175 took one last look at the dying man at his feet, lying in a pool of his own blood, his intestines slithering out on to the ground.

"Why?" he echoed.

Barsch nodded his head weakly, unable to speak now.

"*Revenge*," Smith 175 said and pressed the trigger one last time to blow Barsch's face away.

Envoi

Churchill listened attentively on the phone, nodding his head now and again, as if in agreement with what the person at the other end was saying. Once he exclaimed with apparent enthusiasm, "But how right you are, General!"

At the other end of Churchill's study, the four men, three in uniform and one in civilian clothes, but obviously a soldier, too, sat stiffly at attention and pretended not to listen, which of course they were doing.

"My dear Patton," Churchill said finally, "I do wish to thank you most heartily for your co-operation in that affair in Bavaria. I hope, too, that recovering the bullion will be widely publicised, which it should be. I shall ensure that the London *Times* hears of the matter as soon as Ike releases the information. It will undoubtedly be a feather in your cap. Goodbye, General, and once again many thanks!"

He replaced the phone and sighed before he turned to face his four visitors, saying, "Nothing will save Patton now, of course. I hear from my sources at the General's HQ that Eisenhower is going to fire him this week. Apparently he compared Nazis with the US democrats and republican parties." Churchill chuckled in that mischievous, schoolboyish manner of

213

his. "And perhaps in a way he was right. No matter. He will have to go." He shook his head. "A shame in a way. A good cavalry general. Would have been a good man to have on one's side when we're forced to take on the Russians. No matter, to other things closer to home."*

He stared around their faces: Miles O'Sullivan, Staff Sergeant Smith, a youngster in the uniform of the Parachute Regiment, whose name he didn't know, and ex-Colonel Franks of the SAS, now manager of the Park Lane Hotel, a veteran officer of the Special Air Service. "Colonel Franks, pray introduce me to the young man, whose name I do not know."

Franks, hard-faced and very erect, said, "Sir, this is Private Guy O'Sullivan of the Parachute Regiment. He has just finished his parachute training at Ringway and is being posted to the Sixth Airborne Division in Palestine. But if we pull this thing off, sir, he is very keen to join us. He'll be the fourth member of the O'Sullivans to have been in the regiment, won't he, Miles?"

The boy blushed – he didn't look a day over 17 – and Miles nodded proudly, knowing that his younger cousin was made of the right stuff. He'd make a welcome addition to the SAS if it were ever reformed, though that seemed decidedly unlikely.

Churchill nodded his approval and Guy blushed even more. Then the ex-Prime Minister got down to business. "I have called you here, gentlemen, to tell you that you are not being returned to your regiments."

* After Patton's death in an accident three months later Churchill was the only one of the great statesmen of the Western Alliance ever to visit Patton's grave in Luxembourg. None of America's presidents, including President Eisenhower, has ever done so.

Staff Smith 175 looked relieved. He hadn't fancied going back to all that square-bashing and bull with the Brigade of Guards. He wouldn't have taken to all that 'If it moves, salute it. If it doesn't, paint it white' stuff.

As for his part, Miles O'Sullivan looked puzzled. He had been waiting for a posting in a reinforcement holding unit ever since they had returned from Bavaria. But none had come because the only regiment he had ever belonged to was the SAS.

Churchill turned to the hard-faced ex-commander of the 2nd SAS Regiment and said, "Perhaps you will explain, Franks?"

"Sir," Franks barked, as if he were back at the head of his regiment. He turned his attention to the three men in uniform. "There's a whole bunch of us who were in the SAS living in the Greater London area. We have petitioned the War Office to be allowed to form a territorial squadron of the SAS. We were turned down flat. Too expensive, parachute training and all that—"

"Yes," Churchill interjected sourly. "The new government's too busy paying for granny's teeth and grandad's glasses. As I've said before, the Empire will be lost paying for the Welfare State." He waved his cigar and Franks continued.

"So," Franks allowed himself a tight grin, "we have decided to start a covert operation right here in Britain."

Smith looked impressed and Miles blurted out, "*A covert operation* – what kind, sir?"

"We're all going to join the Artists' Rifles – they've got their drill hall in Duke Street. Very discreet. There we are going to start a new SAS territorial regiment, with the aid of you two, O'Sullivan and Smith, and

215

you too Private O'Sullivan, once you've had a bit of operational experience in Palestine."

"But why us, sir?" Miles asked puzzled. "And how?"

"I shall tell you," Churchill interrupted once again. As always, he never could allow anyone else to talk too long. "You, Captain O'Sullivan, will become the regular army adjutant to the Artists' Rifles and you, Smith, will be promoted to sergeant major, warrant officer class two, and also become the senior non-comissioned officer attached to the Rifles."

"Thank you very much, sir," Miles said, very confused now. "But how can we help an infantry mob – er unit – to train as an SAS one?"

"Like this," Franks took up the story. "Through our connections inside the Army you will make the arrangements for the men to train and fight in the SAS style. This isn't going to be a drill and drink club like most of the pre-war terrier units. This unit is going to train for war – SAS style." His lantern jaw hardened. "And you are the chaps who are going to do the arrangements until the War Office changes its mind and allows us to reform the SAS. By then *we* might be a bit long in the tooth for active field service, but we will have kept the SAS tradition alive and there will be the nucleus of younger trained men ready for covert ops almost immediately. Do you understand?"

Miles looked at his young cousin, Guy. His face glowed with excitement.

Churchill looked pleased at Franks' statement. He clapped his hands. A servant entered bearing a tray with a bottle of champagne on it and five glasses. Churchill, who had never opened a bottle in his life, nodded his head.

The servant opened the champagne with a napkin and began to fill the glasses while Churchill waited expectantly, though it was only 9.30 in the morning. "Courtesy of Colonel Franks and, unwittingly, the Park Lane Hotel," he commented as the servant gravely handed him his glass. He waited till the others had been served. "I give you a toast, gentlemen."

There was a scraping of chairs as they pushed them back and stood up. Churchill's grin broadened even more. He raised his glass to his chest. "*Le roi est mort,*" he announced in his terrible French: "*Vive le roi.* Let it be the same with the Special Air Service. The SAS is dead . . . *LONG LIVE THE SAS!*" He drained his glass in one gulp. Then with an air of finality, he flung the empty glass into the fireplace, a wicked gleam in his faded eyes.

"*THE SAS IS DEAD . . . LONG LIVE THE SAS!*" they echoed. One by one their glasses smashed into the fireplace.

The die had been cast . . .